COLETTE

(1873–1954), was born Sidonie Gabrielle Colette, in the Burgundian village of Saint-Saveur-en-Puisaye. She was educated at the local school where her fluency in composition earned her the role of star pupil. At twenty, Colette was brought to Paris by her first husband, the notorious Henri Gauthier-Villars ('Willy'), who published her first novels (the *Claudine* series, 1900–1903), under his pseudonym. Through him Colette came to know, among others, Proust, Ravel, Debussy, and Fauré. She divorced Willy in 1906 and spent the next six years on the stage. During this time she began an affair with Missy (The Marquise de Belbeuf) which ended when Colette married Henri de Jouvenel (1910), with whom she later had a daughter. They divorced in 1924.

In 1916 Colette dropped the name 'Willy' and as 'Colette' established herself as a major talent with *Chéri* (1920), which she later adapted for the stage, herself playing Léa, the ageing demi-mondaine, and *La Fin de Chéri* (1926). In 1935 Colette married Maurice Goudeket, with whom she lived until her death.

One of the greatest, and most prolific writers in any language, Colette published over fifty books, despite being increasingly crippled by arthritis. These include *The Vagrant* (1912), *Sido* (1929), *The Gentle Libertine* (1931), *The Ripening Seed* (1932) and *Gigi* (1945, later successfully dramatised on Broadway). She was also, at various times, drama critic, fashion columnist, book reviewer, feature writer and woman's page editor of many major French magazines and newspapers.

Colette was the first woman President of the Goncourt Academy and, on her death, the first French woman to be granted the honour of a State funeral.

D0263444

VIRAGO
MODERN
CLASSIC
NUMBER

383

Colette

THE OTHER
WOMAN

*Translated from the French by
Margaret Crosland*

Translated from the French and selected from
La Femme Cachée and *Paysages et Portraits*

Published by VIRAGO PRESS Limited, March 1993
20–23 Mandela Street, Camden Town, London NW1 0HQ

First published in Britain by Peter Owen Limited, 1971

A CIP catalogue record for this book is available from the British Library

Printed in Britain by Cox & Wyman Ltd, Reading, Berks

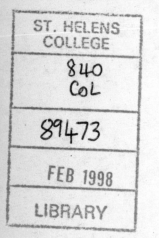

Contents

The Secret Woman

He had been looking for a long time at the sea of masks in front of him, suffering vaguely from their mixture of colours and from the synchronization of two orchestras which were too close. His hood constricted his temples; a nervous headache was coming on between his eyes. But he relished, without impatience, a state of malaise and pleasure which permitted the imperceptible passing of the hours. He had wandered along all the corridors of the Opéra, drunk the silvery dust of the dance-floor, recognized bored friends and placed round his neck the indifferent arms of a very plump girl who was disguised as though humorously as a sylph.

This hooded doctor was embarrassed by his fancy-dress and staggered about like a man in skirts, but he dared not remove either his costume or his hood, because of his school-boy lie :

'I'll be spending tomorrow night at Nogent,' he had said to his wife the day before. 'They've just telephoned me, and I'm very much afraid that my patient, you know, the poor old lady. . . . Just imagine, I was looking forward to this ball like any kid. Isn't it ridiculous, a man of my age who's never been to the Opéra ball?'

'Utterly ridiculous, darling, utterly ! If I'd known, perhaps I wouldn't have married you. . . .'

She laughed, and he admired her narrow face, pink, matt and long, like a delicate sugared almond.

'Don't you want to go to the green and purple ball? Even without me, if it amuses you, darling. . . .'

She had trembled, there passed through her one of those long shudders of disgust which brought a tremble to her hair, her delicate hands and her bosom beneath her white dress whenever she saw a slug or a filthy passer-by :

'As for me. . . . Can you see me in a crowd, at the mercy of all those hands. . . . What do you think, I'm not strait-laced, I'm . . . I'm put out! There's nothing to be done about it!'

Leaning against the loggia balustrade, above the great staircase, he thought of this trembling hind, as he contemplated before him two enormous square hands, with black nails, clasped round the bare back of a sultana. Emerging from the braided sleeves of a Venetian lord they dug into the white female flesh as though it were dough. . . . Because he was thinking of her he jumped violently as he heard beside him a little uh-hum, a kind of cough typical of his wife. . . . He turned round and saw someone sitting astride the balustrade, wearing a long and impenetrable disguise, looking like Pierrot because of the smock with vast sleeves, the loose trousers, the headband and the plaster-white colour which covered the small area of skin visible below the fluffy lace of the mask. The fluid fabric of the costume and the cap, woven of dark purple and silver, shone like the conger-eels that you fish for at night with iron hooks from boats lit by lamps burning resin. Overwhelmed with astonishment he awaited the recurrence of the little uh-hum, which did not come. . . . The eel-like Pierrot remained seated in nonchalant fashion and its heel tapped against the marble baluster, revealing only two satin slippers, while a black-gloved hand lay folded at one hip. The two oblique slits in the mask, carefully meshed over with tulle, revealed only a subdued glint of indeterminate colour.

He almost called out 'Irène!' And restrained himself, remembering his own lie. Since he was clumsy at play-acting he also rejected the idea of disguising his voice. The Pierrot scratched its thigh, with a free, proletarian gesture, and the anxious husband breathed again.

'Ah! It's not her.'

But the Pierrot pulled out of a pocket a flat gold box, opened it and took out a lipstick, and the anxious husband recognized an antique snuff-box fitted with a mirror inside, the last birthday gift. . . . He placed his left hand over the painful area of his heart with such a brusque and involuntary gesture that the eel-like Pierrot noticed him.

'Is that a declaration, purple Domino?'

He did not reply, for he was half stifled with surprise, waiting and nightmare, and listened for a long moment to the barely disguised voice—the voice of his wife. The Eel looked at him, as it sat in cavalier fashion, its head on one side like a bird; it shrugged its shoulders, jumped to the ground and moved away. Its movement liberated the anxious husband who, restored to a state of active and normal jealousy, began to think again and rose without haste to follow his wife.

'She's here for someone, with someone. In less than an hour I'll know everything.'

A hundred hoods, purple or green, guaranteed that he would be neither noticed nor recognized. Irène walked in front of him, nonchalantly; he was astonished to find that she rolled her hips softly and dragged her feet a little as though she were wearing Turkish slippers. A Byzantine figure, wearing emerald green, embroidered with gold, seized her as she went by, and her body bent in his arms; she looked thinner, as though the embrace would cut her in two. Her husband ran a few steps and reached the couple just as Irène was crying flatteringly 'You big brute !'

She moved away, with the same relaxed and quiet step, stopping often, musing at the doors to the open boxes, hardly ever looking round. She hesitated at the foot of the steps, turned off to the side, came back towards the entrance of the orchestra stalls, joined a noisy, closely packed crowd with a skilful gliding movement like the blade of a knife fitting neatly into its sheath. Ten arms imprisoned her, an almost naked wrestler pinned her firmly against the edge of the ground-floor boxes and held her there. She gave way beneath the weight of the naked man, threw back her head in laughter that was drowned by other laughter, and the man in the purple hood saw her teeth gleam beneath the lace of the mask. Then she escaped easily and sat down on the steps which led to the dance-floor. Her husband, standing two paces behind her, looked at her. She readjusted her mask and her crumpled smock, then tightened the headband. She seemed as calm as if she had been alone, and moved away again after a few moments' rest. She went down the steps, placed her hand on the shoulders of a warrior who asked her, silently, to dance, and she danced, clinging to him.

'That's the man,' the husband said to himself.

But she did not say a word to the dancer encased in iron, whose skin was damp, and left him quietly after the dance. She went off to drink a glass of champagne at the buffet, then a second glass, paid, stood by motionless and curious as two men began to fight among screaming women. She also amused herself by placing her little satanic hands, which were entirely black, on the white bosom of a Dutch woman wearing a gold head-dress, who cried out nervously.

At last the anxious man who was following her saw her

stop, as though bumping against him on the way, close to a young man who had collapsed on a bench, out of breath, and was fanning himself with his mask. She bent down, disdainfully held the savage, handsome young face, and kissed the panting, half-open mouth. . . .

But her husband, instead of rushing forward and forcing the two mouths apart, disappeared into the crowd. In his consternation he no longer feared, no longer hoped for betrayal. He was sure now that Irène did not know the young man, drunk with dancing, whom she was kissing, nor the Hercules; he was sure that she was neither waiting nor looking for anyone, and that abandoning the lips she held beneath her own like an empty grape, she was going to leave again the next moment, wander about once more, collect some other passer-by, forget him, and simply enjoy, until she felt tired and went back home, the monstrous pleasure of being alone, free, honest in her crude, native state, of being the unknown woman, eternally solitary and shameless, restored to her irremediable solitude and immodest innocence by a little mask and a concealing costume.

Dawn

The surgical suddenness of their break left him stupefied. Alone in the house where the two of them had lived together in near-conjugal fashion for some twenty years he could not succeed, after a week, in finding grief. He struggled comically against the disappearance of ordinary objects and trounced his valet in childish fashion : 'Those collars can't really have been eaten ! And don't tell me I haven't any more sticks of shaving-soap, there were two in the bathroom cupboard ! You won't make me believe that I haven't any more shaving-soap because Madame isn't here !'

He was terrified by the feeling that he was no longer being organized, he forgot meal-times, came home for no reason, went out in order to escape, mumbled in a half-choked voice into the telephone, which was no longer handed to him in imperious fashion by a woman. He called his friends to witness, embarrassed them and shocked them, whether they were unfaithful or enslaved. 'My dear chap, it's incredible ! Cleverer men than me wouldn't understand it. . . . Aline's gone. She's gone, there it is. And not alone, you understand. She's gone. I could say it a hundred times and find nothing more to add. Apparently these things happen every day to lots of husbands. What can I say ? I can't get over it. No, I can't get over it.'

His eyes would grow round, he would spread out his arms, then let them drop again. He looked neither tragic nor humiliated and his friends despised him slightly : 'He's going downhill. . . . At his age it's been a blow to him.' They talked

18

about him as though he were old, secretly pleased that they could at last belittle this handsome man whose hair was turning slightly grey and who had never had any disappointments in love.

'His beautiful Aline. . . . He found it quite natural that at forty-five she suddenly went blonde, with a complexion like an artificial flower, and that she changed her dressmaker and her shoemaker. He wasn't suspicious. . . .'

One day he took the train; his valet had asked him for a week's leave : 'Since there's less work because Madame's not here, I thought. . . .' And also because he was losing more and more sleep, dozing off at dawn after staying awake like a huntsman on the lookout, motionless in the dark, his jaws clenched and his ears twitching. He left one evening, avoiding the house in the country he had bought fifteen years earlier and furnished for Aline. He took a ticket for a large provincial town where he remembered having acted as spokesman for *L'Extension économique* and banqueted at their expense.

'A good hotel,' he told himself, 'a restaurant with old-style French cooking, that's what I need. I don't want this thing to kill me, do I? All right, let's go away. Travel, good food. . . .'

During the journey the railway-compartment mirror reflected the figure that was still upright and the grey moustache concealing the relaxed mouth. 'Not bad, not bad. Good heavens, it won't kill me ! The minx !' This was the only word he used to insult the unfaithful woman, the moderate, old-fashioned word still used by elderly people to praise the rashness of youth.

At the hotel he asked for the same room he had had the previous year. 'A bay window, you know, with a nice view over the square'; he supped off cold meat and beer and went to bed when the evening was almost over. His exhaustion led him to believe that his flight would be rewarded by prompt sleep. Lying on his back he relished the coolness of the damp sheets, and worked out in the dark the forgotten location of the big bay window, starting from two tall shafts of bluish light between the drawn curtains. In fact he sank quietly to sleep for a few seconds and then woke up for good : he had unconsciously moved his legs back to leave room for her who was now absent day and night but returned faithfully when he slept. He woke up and bravely uttered the conspiratorial words : 'Come now, it'll soon be daylight, be patient.' The two blue shafts of light were turning pink, and from the square he heard the cheerful, rasping din of the iron-hooped wooden buckets and the plonk of the horses' big patient hooves. 'The same sound as the stables at Fontainebleau, exactly what we heard at that villa we'd rented near the hotel. . . . When dawn broke we used to listen. . . .' He shuddered, turned over and once more sought sleep. The horses and the buckets were quiet now. Other sounds, more discreet, came up through the open window. He distinguished the solid, muffled sound of flower-pots being unloaded from a van, a sound like light rain as the plants were watered, and the gentle thud as large armfuls of leaves were thrown down on to the ground.

'A flower-market,' said the sleepless man to himself. 'Oh, I can't be mistaken about it. In Strasbourg during that trip we made, the early morning revealed a delightful flower-market beneath our windows, and she said she had never seen such blue cinerarias as. . . .' He sat up, in order to combat more effectively a mood of despair whose tide flowed in regular waves, a new kind of despair, quite different, unknown. Beneath the nearby bridge, oars struck the sleeping river and the flight of the first swallows whistled through the air : 'It's early morning at Como, the swallows behind the gardener's boat, the smell of fruit and vegetables came through our windows at the Villa d'Este. . . . God be merciful. . . .' He still had the strength to blush as he started a prayer, although the pain of loneliness and memory left him hunched up on his bed like a man with tuberculosis. Twenty years . . . all the dawns of twenty years poured over the companion, sleeping or wakeful at his side, their faint or brilliant ray of light, their bird-call, their pearly raindrops, twenty years. . . .

'I don't want it to kill me, damn it. Twenty years, it's a long time. But before her I knew other dawns. . . . So let's see, when I was a very young man. . . .'

But he could resurrect only the half-light known to poor students, the grey mornings at the law school warmed by skimmed milk or alcohol, mornings in furnished rooms with narrow wash-basins or zinc buckets. He turned away from them, invoked the aid of his adolescence and the dawns of that time, but they came to him cringing and bitter, rising from a rickety iron bed, prisoners of a wretched time, marked on the cheek by a violent blow, dragging shoes with rotten soles. . . . The abandoned man realized that there was no escape for him and that he would struggle in vain against the returning light, that the cruel and familiar harmony of the first hour of the day would sing one name only, reopen one wound only, each time recent and renewed; then he went down into bed again and obediently burst into tears.

One Evening

The iron gate closed again and the lantern carried by one of the gardeners began to dance up and down in front of us, while only a few drops from the heavy shower reached us through a covert of clipped yews. We felt that shelter was near, and we agreed laughingly that the car breakdown which had just stopped us in the middle of the countryside was certainly in the category of happy accidents.

It happened in fact that Monsieur B. . . , owner of the château and county councillor by profession, who greeted the two rain-soaked and unexpected women travellers on the stone steps, knew my husband slightly and that his wife—a former pupil of the *Schola cantorum*—remembered having met me at Sunday concerts.

We became very gay and talkative beside the first wood-fire of the season. My friend Valentine and I had to accept the pot-luck meal of cold meat washed down with champagne; our hosts had barely finished dinner.

Old plum brandy and steaming hot coffee made us feel almost intimate. The electric light, which was rare in this district, the smell of mild tobacco, fruit, and the blazing resinous wood—I relished these familiar delights like gifts offered by some unknown island.

Monsieur B. . . , who was square-set and barely going grey, with a charming southern-type smile which showed his white teeth, occupied my friend Valentine, and I looked at Madame B. . . more than I spoke to her.

She was fair, slim and dressed more suitably for a smart

dinner party than for receiving stray motorists; I was surprised by her eyes, so light in colour that the faintest gleam
of brightness robbed them of their pale blue. They became
mauve like her dress, green like the silk cover on the armchair, or disturbed, through the light from the lamp, with
fleeting, clouded moiré streaks like the blue eyes of a Siamese
cat.

I wondered if these over-light coloured eyes did not give
the face its absent-minded air, its empty amiability, its often
somnambulistic smile. She was in any case a somnambulist
singularly attentive to everything that could please us and
shorten the two or three hours that our chauffeur, assisted by
Monsieur B. . .'s mechanic, would need to repair the car.

'We have a room available for you,' Madame B. . . said to
me. 'Why not spend the night here?'

And her eyes, as though abandoned, expressed only un-
limited and almost unthinking solitude.

'You're not too uncomfortable here, now, are you,' she
went on. 'Look at my husband, how well he's getting on with
your friend!'

She laughed, and her wide-open, deserted eyes did not
seem to listen to her words. Twice she asked me to repeat
some trivial phrase, starting slightly on each occasion. Was
it morphine? Or opium? A drug-taker would never have had
those rosy gums, that relaxed brow, that gentle warm hand,
nor that full, elastic flesh below the *décolleté* neckline.

Was I dealing with the silent victim of a conjugal situation? No. A tyrant, even Machiavellian in type, never says
'Simone' so tenderly, never bestows such a flattering look
upon his slave. . . .

'Yes, Madame,' Monsieur B. . . was just saying to my
friend Valentine, 'they *do* exist, there are married couples

who live in the country for eight months of the year, are never out of each other's sight and don't complain! Isn't that so, Simone, they do exist, don't they?'

'Thank goodness, yes,' replied Simone.

And her eyes, which were barely blue, contained nothing, nothing except a minute yellow spark, very far away—the reflection of the lamp in the protruding side of a samovar. Then she stood up and poured us a cup of steaming hot tea flavoured with rum 'for the night drive'. It was ten o'clock. A young man came in, bare-headed, and before any introduction was made he gave a few opened letters to Monsieur B. . . , who asked Valentine to excuse him and rapidly went through his correspondence.

'My husband's secretary,' explained Madame B. . . , who was cutting a lemon into thin slices.

I said what was in my mind : 'He's good-looking.'

'Do you think so?'

She raised her eyebrows like a woman saying with surprise 'I've never thought about it'. However, this slim young man, in no way self-conscious, was striking because of his air of obstinacy, his habit of lowering his eyelids which meant that when he raised them his expression was more remarkable through the brusque, violent, swiftly removed glance that was more disdainful than shy. He accepted a cup of tea and sat by the fire, near Madame B. . . , thus taking the second place on one of those ugly, useful S-shaped seats in 1880 style called *causeuses*.

There was a moment of silence and I was afraid we had tired such pleasant hosts.

'How comfortable it all is !' I murmured, in order to break the silence. 'I shall remember this delightful house, which I've lived in for one evening without knowing what it looks like from the outside. . . . This fire will still warm us, won't it, Valentine, if we close our eyes against the wind . . . later. . . .'

'That will really be your fault,' cried Madame B. . . . 'If it were me, I wouldn't need any sympathy, I love driving at night, with the rain streaking across the headlights, and drops on people's cheeks like tears. Oh, I love it all !'

I looked at her with surprise. Her whole person shone with a delicious human flame which had perhaps been stifled by shyness during the first hours. She didn't hold back any more and her attractive confidence revealed her as gay and discriminating, well informed about local politics and her husband's ambitions, which she laughed at by speaking like he did, as young girls do when they are play-acting. There was no lamp on the chimney-piece and only the crackling hearth, a long way from the central light, lent colour or shade to this young woman whose sudden animation made me think of the gaiety of canaries when the lamps are lit and wake them up in their cages. I could see Monsieur B. . .'s secretary from the back, in his dark jacket, as he leant at an angle against the S-shaped arm-rest which separated him from Madame B. . . . While she was talking to her husband and my friend, turning towards them from a slight distance away, I rose to put down my empty cup and I saw that the young man's concealed hand was clasping Madame B. . .'s bare arm in a firm and completely motionless embrace, above the elbow. Neither of them moved, in his visible hand the young man held a cigarette he was not smoking, and Madame B. . . was waving a small fan. She was talking happily, attentive to everyone, her eyes limpid, in a voice occasionally interrupted by more rapid breathing, as though she wanted to laugh, and I could see the veins swelling on one of her hands as the grip on it became so loving and hard.

Like someone who feels he is being looked at, Monsieur B. . .'s secretary suddenly rose, said goodbye to us all and left.

'Can't I hear the sound of our motor?' I asked Madame B. . . a moment later.

She didn't reply. She was looking at the fire, inclining her head towards a faint sound and her air of slight collapse made her look like a woman who has just had a rather severe fall. I repeated my question; she started : 'Yes, yes, I think so . . .' she said suddenly.

Her eyelids flickered, bestowing on me a smile of rigid grace, and her eyes were possessed once again by the cold and the void : 'What a pity !'

We left, taking with us autumn roses and black dahlias. Monsieur B. . . walked beside the car, which started slowly, as far as the first bend in the drive. Madame B. . . stood on the lighted steps, smiling at us, her face abandoned by the passing certainty of living; one of her hands moved up beneath her transparent scarf and clasped her bare arm above the elbow.

The Hand

He had fallen asleep on his young wife's shoulder, and she
proudly supported the weight of his head, with its fair hair,
his sanguine-complexioned face and closed eyes. He had
slipped his large arm beneath the slim, adolescent back and
his strong hand lay flat on the sheet, beside the young
woman's right elbow. She smiled as she looked at the man's
hand emerging there, quite alone and far removed from its
owner. Then she let her glance stray round the dimly lit bedroom. A conch-shaped lamp threw a subdued glow of peri-
winkle-blue over the bed. 'Too happy to sleep,' she thought.

Too excited also, and often surprised by her new state. For
only two weeks she had taken part in the scandalous existence of a honeymoon couple, each of them relishing the
pleasure of living with an unknown person they were in love
with. To meet a good-looking, fair-haired young man,
recently widowed, good at tennis and sailing, and marry him
a month later : her conjugal romance fell little short of
abduction. Whenever she lay awake beside her husband,
like tonight, she would still keep her eyes closed for a long
time, then open them and relish with astonishment the blue
of the brand-new curtains, replacing the apricot-pink which
had filtered with the morning light into the room where she
had slept as a girl.

A shudder ran through the sleeping body lying beside her
and she tightened her left arm round her husband's neck,
with the delightful authority of weak creatures. He did not
wake up.

27

'What long eyelashes he has,' she said to herself.

She silently praised also the full, graceful mouth, the brick-red skin and the forehead, neither noble nor lofty, but still free of wrinkles.

Her husband's right hand, beside her, also shuddered, and beneath the curve of her back she felt the right arm, on which her whole weight was resting, come to life.

'I'm heavy . . . I'd like to reach up and put the light out, but he's so fast asleep. . . .'

The arm tensed again, gently, and she arched her back to make herself lighter.

'It's as though I were lying on an animal,' she thought.

She turned her head slightly on the pillow and looked at the hand lying beside her.

'How big it is! It's really bigger than my whole head!'

The light which crept from under the edge of a blue crystal globe fell on to this hand and showed up the slightest reliefs in the skin, exaggerated the powerful, knotty knuckles and the veins which stood out because of the pressure on the arm. A few russet hairs, at the base of the fingers, all lay in the same direction, like ears of wheat in the wind, and the flat nails, whose ridges had not been smoothed out by the polisher, gleamed beneath their coat of pink varnish.

'I'll tell him not to put varnish on his nails,' thought the young wife. 'Varnish and carmine don't suit a hand so . . . a hand so . . .'

An electric shock ran through the hand and spared the young woman the trouble of thinking of an adjective. The thumb stiffened until it was horribly long and spatulate, and moved close up against the index finger. In this way the hand suddenly acquired an apelike appearance.

'Oh!' said the young woman quietly, as though faced with some minor indecency.

The horn of a passing car pierced the silence with a noise so shrill that it seemed luminous. The sleeper did not wake but the hand seemed offended and reared up, tensing itself like a crab and waiting for the fray. The piercing sound receded and the hand, gradually relaxing, let fall its claws, became a soft animal, bent double and shaken with faint jerks which looked like a death agony. The flat, cruel nail on the over-long thumb glistened. On the little finger there appeared a slight deviation which the young woman had never noticed, and the sprawling hand revealed its fleshy palm like a red belly.

'And I've kissed that hand! . . . How horrible! I can't ever have looked at it!'

The hand was disturbed by some bad dream, and seemed to respond to this sudden reaction, this disgust. It regrouped its forces, opened out wide, spread out its tendons, its nerves and its hairiness like a panoply of war. Then it slowly withdrew, grasped a piece of sheeting, dug down with its curving fingers and squeezed and squeezed with the methodical pleasure of a strangler. . . .

'Oh!' cried the young woman.

The hand disappeared, the large arm was freed of its burden and in one moment became a protective girdle, a warm bulwark against the terrors of night. But next morning, when the tray with frothing chocolate and toast was on the bed, she saw the hand again, russet and red, and the ghastly thumb crooked over the handle of a knife.

'Do you want this piece of toast, darling? I'm doing it for you.'

She shuddered and felt gooseflesh high up on her arms and down her back.

'Oh, no . . . no . . .'

Then she concealed her fear, controlled herself bravely and, beginning her life of duplicity, resignation, base and subtle diplomacy, she leant over and humbly kissed the monstrous hand.

The Dead End

He had taken the long, magnificent blonde, who looked like a bloodhound on a lead, from another man. He had followed her everywhere, approached her in romantic fashion and carried her off. They did not even know what had become of the other man and never found out. The loser accepted his defeat in honourable fashion and ceased to exist for them. The winner—let us call him Armand and the woman Elsie—gave him little thought, for Elsie loved *him*; and, moreover, he concerned himself only with proving his love and his naïveté by organizing that prison called life together. She helped him do it, flattered like all women whom people claim they are imprisoning with love. A few weeks of hotels and travelling ended naturally in a lakeside villa where they sincerely thought they would find the abode of happiness.

A kind of laziness, care for her beauty and the slowness of her movements shortened the hours of the day for Elsie. Those of the night, given over to sleep or love, seemed short. Since they had both stated, in due time, that between lovers silence is golden, they could remain silent without impunity until further notice. They never went out, came home or wandered through the woods except together, leaning against one another, or he walking behind her, while she trailed behind her a ribbon, one end of a veil, or part of a dress, like a lead which had been broken.

Away from Paris they had no difficulty in ensuring their isolation; the spectacle of love is enough to drive away the best of friends. One can seek out a man who is infatuated, a woman in love—but associating with a happy couple who show their happiness, is tedious, offensive to our taste for moderate diversions and healthy harmony.

So they lived together, on their own, with the unconscious and stupid bravura of lovers. On certain days at twilight, when the clouds are low, the wind drops and a storm is brewing, when the whole of nature broods over a tragedy, she was not afraid to find this stranger before her, with his broad shoulders, fierce eyebrows and prompt movements. For deep within herself a woman retains the confidence she has in her ravisher.

Armand hardly thought about the woman's past, for he held her close to him night and day, and the past of her whom he loved was completely unknown to him. Elsie's past, for Armand, was a poor man, disappointed and swallowed up in darkness and oblivion. He sometimes wondered, dutifully as it were, 'But what happened before that poor man?' and returned quickly to the present which had neither clouds nor secrets.

The suffering overtook him one morning when he was looking at the lake and the pink pewter mist which lay over it, behind a hedge ablaze with crimson geraniums, and Elsie was singing to herself, on the first floor of the house, as she dressed. He realized that he did not know the song, and that Elsie had never sung it before. He was surprised, and conjectured that she was thinking, as she sang, of a time that was past, of people with names unknown to him, perhaps of an unknown man. . . .

When his mistress rejoined him he found her slightly different from the woman he had been expecting, and told her so with tender solicitude. She replied, unsuspectingly, that the first rains of autumn made her feel cold, and she talked about stoves, big wood-fires and furs with an air of covetousness and coquettish fear. Then he stopped looking at her and, lowering his eyes, began to add up the months they had just passed together, and he thought that perhaps she wanted to go. . . . The image he formed of Elsie's absence took him back to the time when he lived without her, and he trembled at the thought that, during that distant time, he had been capable of living another life. He looked up at Elsie again and his heart did not melt with love but beat hard and painfully, for he thought : 'I've been a man like other men. Elsie's a woman like other women, except that she's more beautiful. The man I took her from has certainly gone back to being like other men, a man deprived of happiness, a normal, sad, frivolous man. The man who will come after me. . . .'

He stumbled mentally, stopped reasoning and saw that he was entering abjectly into that state of aimless jealousy which innocence does not cure.

He concealed his pain as best he could, while redoubling affectionate demands. But the care he employed to subdue the thought at the back of his mind overwhelmed him with mental fatigue which quickly reached his perceptive mistress. He struggled, sure of his expression and his words, and it was Elsie who suffered from uneasiness, yawned nervously, trembled as she saw, one moonlit evening, Armand's shadow, standing there expressive and alive like a third person. . . . He noticed her weaknesses, put them down to regret, the desire to escape, and one day fiercely insulted his mistress, who was reassured and filled with pride by this outburst.

Within himself he grumbled : 'Yes, prison . . . the harem with bolted doors. . . .'

But at the same time he was doubtful of any remedy and,

although anxious for a few moments of separation, he felt no gratitude at the reappearance of her whom he could not manage without. He now looked for faults in her and in his anxiety for peace of mind he willed the marks of age upon her, but when she looked less beautiful one day than the day before and the day after he hated her for seeming to obey his hostile wishes.

He lived in that aberration of mind which punishes those whom love has abused by urging them to begin the earthly paradise all over again. He even tried to go away from Elsie on futile pretexts, but each time he came back more agitated and more vindictive, for he was not away long enough to set foot on the land of normal sorrow, the sorrow of privation, and his relief at having left his mistress would yield immediately to the intolerable supposition that she had run away during his absence.

*

One day when he had left Elsie at the villa and was walking alone by the edge of the lake, submitting his aberration to a kind of discipline without hope, he heard someone running behind him; turning round, he saw one of Elsie's servants, looking strangely upset. She stopped, breathlessly, a few paces away from him.

'Oh, Monsieur . . . Madame . . .'

'Madame?' he called out, in a loud, artificial voice. 'Yes? She's just left, hasn't she?'

The servant opened her mouth, closed it, could say nothing for a moment, then uttered a few words from which the man understood that an accident . . . a fall on the marble steps . . . a fractured skull . . . instantaneous death . . . death. . . . Feeling relaxed, he sat down on the grass.

'Oh,' he sighed, 'I was afraid. . . .'

The Fox

The man who takes his fox for a walk in the Bois de Boulogne is certainly a fine fellow. He thinks he's giving pleasure to the little fox, who was probably his companion in the trenches and whom he tamed to the terrible sound of bombardments. The man with the fox, followed by his captive like a dog on a chain, is unaware that out in the open, in surroundings which might remind him of his native forest, the fox is no more than a stray spirit full of despair, an animal blinded by the light he had forgotten, intoxicated by scents, ready to rush forward, to attack or flee—but an animal with a collar round his neck. Apart from these details, the good little tame fox loves his master and follows him with his belly close to the ground and his fine tail, the colour of slightly burnt toast, hanging down low. He laughs readily— a fox is always laughing. He has beautiful velvet eyes—like all foxes—and I can find nothing more to say about him.

The other fine fellow, the man with the hens, would emerge about half past eleven from the Auteuil métro. Over his shoulder he carried a bag of dark fabric, rather like the bag of crusts that tramps carry, and at a brisk pace he would reach the tranquil glades of Auteuil. The first time I saw him he had placed his mysterious bag on a bench and waited for me to go away with my dogs. I reassured him and he carefully shook his bag, from which there fell a cock and a hen, both with gleaming red crests and autumn-coloured plumage; without wasting a moment they pecked and scraped at the cool moss and the forest humus. I asked no unnecessary questions and the hen-man gave me a brief explanation : 'I bring them out at midday whenever I can. It's only fair, isn't it . . . when birds live in an apartment. . . .'

I replied with a compliment about the beauty of the handsome cock and the liveliness of the hen; I added that I was also acquainted with the little girl who brought her big tortoise to 'play' in the afternoons, and with the fox-man. . . .

'He's no acquaintance of mine,' said the hen-man. . . .

But chance was to bring together the owner of the fox and the owner of the hens, along one of those paths sought out by solitary-minded people guided by their fear of keepers and the fancy of a dog, a fox or a hen. At first the fox-man did not reveal himself. He sat in the thicket, holding his fox in paternal fashion round the middle of his serpentine body, and was touched when he found him rigid with attention. The fox's nervous laugh bared his sharp canine teeth, slightly yellow from idleness and soft food, while his white whiskers, which lay quite flat against his cheeks, looked as though they had been touched up with cosmetics.

A few yards away the cock and the hen, satiated with grain, were taking their sand-bath in the sunshine. The cock passed his iron beak over the feathers in his wings, and the hen, puffed up in the shape of an egg, her feet invisible and her crop extended, was covering herself in dust as yellow as pollen. A faint discordant cry uttered by the cock awoke her. She preened herself and then walked unsteadily over to her husband.

'What did you say?' she asked.

He must have made a sign to her, for she didn't argue and stood by him, as close to the bag as possible—the bag, the prison without a trap. . . .

However, the hen-man, who was astonished by this behaviour, reassured his birds by uttering 'Dearrs, dearrs!' and familiar onomatopoeic sounds.

A few days later the fox-man, who thought he was doing the right thing in offering this tantalizing pleasure to his little wild animal, decided it would be fair to reveal his presence and that of his fox.

'Oh, they're peculiar animals,' said the hen-man.

'And intelligent,' said the fox-man, going further. 'And they don't mean any harm. If you gave him your hen, he wouldn't know what to do with her.'

But the little fox shuddered, with an imperceptible and passionate shudder, under his fur, while the cock and the hen, who were reassured by the sound of friendly voices— and they were also stupid—pecked and clucked beneath the fox's velvet eye.

The two animal-lovers became friendly, as people become friendly in the Bois or at a spa. You meet, you chat, you tell your favourite story, you tell the person you don't know two or three confidential things unknown to your close friends— and then you separate by the No. 16 tram-stop—without giving either the name of the street where you live or the number of your house.

A little fox, even when he's deprived, could not be near hens without experiencing grave qualms. He grew thin, and dreamt aloud all night, in his yelping language. And his master, as he watched the fox's delicate and feverish muzzle turn away from his saucer of milk, saw coming towards him, from the depths of a green thicket in Auteuil, a wicked thought, barely distinct, with a moving shape that was faint but already ugly. . . . That day he chatted in a good friendly way with his friend the hen-man and absent-mindedly slackened the fox's chain a little, the fox took a step—should

I call it a step, the gliding that neither revealed the tip of his toes nor crushed a single blade of grass—towards the hen.

'Hey there!' exclaimed the hen-man.

'Oh!' said the fox-man, 'he wouldn't touch it.'

'I know that,' said the hen-man.

The fox said nothing. He was pulled back and sat down sensibly while his glittering eyes expressed no thought.

The next day the two friends exchanged views about line-fishing.

'If it was cheaper,' said the hen-man, 'I'd get a licence for the Upper Lake. But it's expensive. It makes roach more expensive than at the central market.'

'But it's worth it,' the fox-man replied. 'A chap by the little lake caught so much the other day! Twenty-eight roach and a bream bigger than my hand.'

'Fancy that!'

'And then, without blowing my own trumpet, I'm not so bad either. You should see me cast a line . . . I know how to flick my wrist, you know. . . . Like this. . . .'

He stood up, let go the fox's chain and whirled his arm in masterly fashion. A frenzied, russet object streaked through the grass in the direction of the yellow hen, but the hen-man quickly shot out his leg to stop him and there was only a muffled little bark. The fox went back to his master's feet and lay down.

'That was a near thing . . .' said the hen-man.

'I'm really very surprised,' said the fox-man. 'Will you say sorry to the gentleman, at once, boy? What are you up to, then?' . . .

The hen-man looked his friend in the eye and there read his secret, his unformed, pale and wicked thought. . . . He coughed, feeling choked with angry blood coming suddenly into his throat, and almost flew at the fox-man, who said to himself at the same moment, 'The devil take him, him and his backyard. . . .' They both made the same effort to return to ordinary life, lowered their heads and moved away from each other, for ever, in the cautious fashion of honest folk who had just been within an inch of committing murder.

The Judge

When Madame de La Hournerie came home, after half a day devoted entirely to the hairdresser and the milliner, she quickly tossed away her new hat in order to examine her new hair-style. Following skilful solicitations from Anthèlme, who called himself the fashionable hairdresser, she had just abandoned her 1910 style chignon, the bouffant waves of her beautiful mahogany-coloured hair, appropriate to a fifty-year-old woman, along with the flowing tress and the curls which shadowed her forehead and ears. She had come home with the same mahogany colour, but with her hair drawn up in Chinese style, smoothed flat, brilliantined, knotted in a varnished loop at the nape of her neck and transfixed, like a heart, with a little gleaming arrow.

In front of the mirror framed with unshaded lights she started slightly at this steep forehead which she rarely saw and concealed more carefully than a breast, at the hard glare of her eyes, skilfully made up but reached by the light, which robbed them of their mystery, like the sun shining on the forest spring after the woodcutter has been. She took a hand-mirror and admired the large knob of polished hair and the arrow of brilliants at the back of her neck.

'I must say, it's smart,' she said aloud to reassure herself. 'And Emilie de Séry told me just now that I was a real revelation. . . .'

But faced by this lady with the lacquered skull, the slightly sunken broad cheeks, loose mouth and enlarged nose, she did not recognize herself and felt uneasy. With the art of a

painter who enhances the colour of a landscape flooded by
sudden sunshine, she added some rouge to her bare ears, her
temples and under her eyebrows, covering her entire face
with a shade of pink powder that she rarely used.

'That's better,' she decided. 'Obviously it's a daring
hair-style. Why shouldn't I wear a daring hair-style after
all?'

She rang, and received the doubtful compliments of her
lady's maid : 'Everything that changes Madame improves
her a great deal', changed her town clothes and went down
to dine alone. In her elegant widowhood, which had lasted
for five years, she was not afraid of a few hours' solitude, and
Madame de La Hournerie frequently dined and lunched
alone, as a form of salutary and pleasant mortification, just
as she would have absorbed yoghourt or gone to bed at five
o'clock in the afternoon.

Marien, in evening dress, was waiting for her, his arms
dangling, in front of one of his dressers. He was the pride of
the La Hournerie household, six feet tall, with a neat head,
fair hair, fair skin and the black eyes of a fanatical Breton.
When he was thirteen Madame de La Hournerie and her
husband had removed him from the fifty cows that he was
looking after in the fields. Marien, promoted 'junior servant',
given a long-sleeved striped waistcoat and a white apron,
soon earned his stripes. He overcame his terror of the telephone, showed taste in arranging flowers in the vases and on
the table-cloth, muffled his peasant voice and learned to walk
with catlike tread. Later, when he changed the footman's
braided suit for the black frock-coat of the *maître d'hôtel*, a
sort of instinct for conventional manners also taught him to
add only a little to the price of fruit, cut flowers, cleaning
materials and products for polishing all kinds of metals.

Because of this Madame de La Hournerie awarded him prematurely the supreme grade of 'pearl', usually reserved for servants who had become white-haired and feeble. But Marien, an athletic statue of silence, never learnt to extinguish the expressive fire of his severe black eyes, mirrors for soubrettes, stars whose fire would devastate haberdashery shop-girls or women news-vendors.

Madame de La Hournerie entered the dining-room briskly, sat down and shivered : 'Serve me quickly, Marien. It's not warm here, is it?'

Marien, standing in front of the dresser, had not yet moved.

'Well, little one, did I say something?' said Madame de La Hournerie in a familiar way, for she still sometimes treated Marien, kindly, as a 'little valet'.

'The stove's at eighty, though,' an uncertain voice replied at last.

Madame de La Hournerie, who felt the cold in two recently exposed sensitive places—her forehead and her ears —looked up at Marien, who seemed to lose countenance, emptied the full soup ladle into the soup plate, served Madame de La Hournerie, and took up his traditional place again, upright, facing his mistress. The *maître d'hôtel*'s dark eyes, starting out of his head, contemplated, with an indescribable expression of horror and shame, the vast bare forehead, marble-white in colour, and the skull-cap of waxed hair, which matched the red mahogany of the Empire furniture. Madame de La Hournerie was embarrassed and pushed her soup away.

'Give me the next course, Marien. I'm not very hungry. I wouldn't be surprised if I had a touch of flu.'

Marien removed the soup, rushed towards the pantry as

though he were running away and brought in a shrimp
soufflé. As he served it he chipped the edge of an old plate,
spilt a few drops of red wine on the table-cloth, then regained
his dresser and reassumed his shocked contemplation.

'There's flu about,' went on Madame de La Hournerie,
feeling uneasy. . . . 'Take care in the kitchen. . . . Henriette
was complaining this morning that she ached all over. . . .
Take this soufflé away, the shrimps are dried up. . . . And
you haven't got your mind on your work this evening. . . .'

'It's the season for flu,' said the same uncertain voice. . . .

But Marien's black eyes, merciless and truthful, cried out
between each course to Madame de La Hournerie, 'No, it's
not the season for flu. It's this shocking forehead, this pallid
steppe, this over-small skull, this heavy hanging fruit : an old
woman's head stripped of the foliage where I was used to
seeing it ripen ! It's the indignation I feel as an upstanding
scrounger, for I'm attached to the domain I develop and
care for : it's the astonishment of a former little valet who
served a beautiful mistress, a little herdsman devoted to a
dazzling memory. It's not done, my goodness, it's not
done !'

The chocolate trifle bathed in its thick vanilla-flavoured
cream was hardly more successful than the lamb chop and
the artichoke hearts. Madame de La Hournerie, in a state of
exasperation, wanted to react against the importunate and
silent disapproval; a trace of red powder remaining on the
chasing of a fork, the brown marks on the rim of a lamp-
shade, gave her the opportunity. But, paralysed with shame
before the first words of reprimand, she left the table and
ordered drily 'Send Henriette up to me', ran to her boudoir
and sat down in front of the triple mirror. . . .

'Is that you, Henriette? As soon as possible, tomorrow, you

will telephone to Anthèlme, yes, the hairdresser. . . . I want an appointment before luncheon, you understand? before luncheon. . . .'

The Other Wife

'For two? This way, Monsieur and Madame, there's still a table by the bay window, if Madame and Monsieur would like to enjoy the view.'

Alice followed the *maître d'hôtel*.

'Oh, yes, come on Marc, we'll feel we're having lunch on a boat at sea . . .'

Her husband restrained her, passing his arm through hers.

'We'll be more comfortable there.'

'There? In the middle of all those people? I'd much prefer . . .'

'Please, Alice.'

He tightened his grip in so emphatic a way that she turned round.

'What's the matter with you?'

He said 'sh' very quietly, looking at her intently, and drew her towards the table in the middle.

'What is it, Marc?'

'I'll tell you, darling. Let me order lunch. Would you like shrimps? Or eggs in aspic?'

'Whatever *you* like, as you know.'

They smiled at each other, wasting the precious moments of an overworked, perspiring *maître d'hôtel* who stood near to them, suffering from a kind of St Vitus's dance.

'Shrimps,' ordered Marc. 'And then eggs and bacon. And cold chicken with cos lettuce salad. Cream cheese? *Spécialité de la maison*? We'll settle for the *spécialité*. Two very strong coffees. Please give lunch to my chauffeur, we'll be leaving again at two o'clock. Cider? I don't trust it. . . . Dry champagne.'

He sighed as though he had been moving a wardrobe, gazed at the pale noonday sea, the nearly white sky, then at his wife, finding her pretty in her little Mercury-type hat with its long hanging veil.

'You're looking well, darling. And all this sea-blue colour gives you green eyes, just imagine! And you put on weight when you travel. . . . It's nice, up to a point, but only up to a point!'

Her rounded bosom swelled proudly as she leant over the table.

'Why did you stop me taking that place by the bay window?'

It did not occur to Marc Séguy to tell a lie.

'Because you'd have sat next to someone I know.'

'And whom I don't know?'

'My ex-wife.'

She could not find a word to say and opened her blue eyes wider.

'What of it, darling? It'll happen again. It's not important.'

Alice found her tongue again and asked the inevitable questions in their logical sequence.

'Did she see you? Did she know that you'd seen her? Point her out to me.'

'Don't turn round at once, I beg you, she must be looking at us. A lady with dark hair, without a hat, she must be staying at this hotel. . . . On her own, behind those children in red . . .'

'Yes, I see.'

Sheltered behind broad-brimmed seaside hats, Alice was

able to look at the woman who fifteen months earlier had still been her husband's wife. 'Incompatibility,' Marc told her. 'Oh, it was total incompatibility! We divorced like well-brought-up people, almost like friends, quietly and quickly. And I began to love you, and you were able to be happy with me. How lucky we are that in our happiness there haven't been any guilty parties or victims!'

The woman in white, with her smooth, lustrous hair over which the seaside light played in blue patches, was smoking a cigarette, her eyes half closed. Alice turned back to her husband, took some shrimps and butter and ate composedly.

'Why didn't you ever tell me,' she said after a moment's silence, 'that she had blue eyes too?'

'But I'd never thought about it!'

He kissed the hand that she stretched out to the bread basket and she blushed with pleasure. Dark-skinned and plump, she might have seemed slightly earthy, but the changing blue of her eyes, and her wavy golden hair, disguised her as a fragile and soulful blonde. She showed overwhelming gratitude to her husband. She was immodest without knowing it and her entire person revealed over-conspicuous signs of extreme happiness.

They ate and drank with good appetite and each thought that the other had forgotten the woman in white. However, Alice sometimes laughed too loudly and Marc was careful of his posture, putting his shoulders back and holding his head up. They waited some time for coffee, in silence. An incandescent stream, a narrow reflection of the high and invisible sun, moved slowly over the sea and shone with unbearable brilliance.

'She's still there, you know,' Alice whispered suddenly.

'Does she embarrass you? Would you like to have coffee somewhere else?'

'Not at all! It's she who ought to be embarrassed! And she doesn't look as though she's having a madly gay time, if you could see her ...'

'It's not necessary. I know that look of hers.'

'Oh, was she like that?'

He breathed smoke through his nostrils and wrinkled his brows.

'Was she like that? No. To be frank, she wasn't happy with me.'

'Well, my goodness!'

'You're delightfully generous, darling, madly generous. ... You're an angel, you're. ... You love me ... I'm so proud, when I see that look in your eyes ... yes, the look you have now. ... She. ... No doubt I didn't succeed in making her happy. That's all there is to it, I didn't succeed.'

'She's hard to please!'

Alice fanned herself irritably, and cast brief glances at the woman in white who was smoking, her head leaning against the back of the cane chair, her eyes closed with an expression of satisfied lassitude.

Marc shrugged his shoulders modestly.

'That's it,' he admitted. 'What can one do? We have to be sorry for people who are never happy. As for us, we're so happy. ... Aren't we, darling?'

She didn't reply. She was looking with furtive attention at her husband's face, with its good colour and regular shape, at his thick hair, with its occasional thread of white silk, at his small, well-cared-for hands. She felt dubious for the first time, and asked herself: 'What more did she want, then?'

And until they left, while Marc was paying the bill, asking about the chauffeur and the route, she continued to watch, with envious curiosity, the lady in white, that discontented, hard-to-please, superior woman. . . .

The Burglar

It was so easy to get into the little villa that the burglar wondered why, and through what excessive caution, he had waited so long. As soon as he was in the hall he noticed the gloomy dampness that permeates seaside villas during rainy summers. He found the drawing-room door open on to the ante-room, the dining-room door open too, while the cellar door gaped under the stairs, proving the haste with which the little red-haired maid he had just been watching had left for a dance-hall or some hollow in the dunes. One servant only, and a little thing at that : quite enough for Madame Cassart and her tiny villa of pink plaster and green mosaic, standing in a sandy garden where the scrawny tamarisks bowed to the wind from the sea, all facing in the same direction like long-stemmed grasses in water.

The burglar closed the open doors carefully; he didn't like banging doors and was relying on a rapid visit to this ugly plaything rented for the season by Madame Cassart. He had a quick look at the drawing-room—white lacquer and *toile de Jouy*—the tenant wouldn't think of hiding her savings there.

The man walked about easily without any light, assisted by the glimmering darkness, twilight-grey in colour, which forced its way through the lowered Venetian blinds. Only once did he risk the electric beam from his pocket torch, which fell on the photograph of a very beautiful woman, wearing a long corset, her hair fastened up in a 'figure of eight', and evening gloves.

'Cassart in her good days. She's changed.'

For a fortnight he had been in this fishing port, which had become ambitious and endowed with a sudden casino in fibro-cement, living the austere life of an entomologist, studying the ways of life and the habits of the bathers, especially the women, noting the times when they went out, their daily visits to the children's hobby-horses and the dance-hall. The only profits, since his arrival, were a purse full of gold, a commonplace ring left on a wash-basin, and a reticule containing a hundred francs; meagre rewards for his conscientious existence, which aspired to perfection. He dressed correctly and frequented the casino, trying to be as inconspicuous as possible, and made no acquaintances, for he was confident of his demeanour, that of a handsome forty-year-old with close-cropped hair, but knew the weaknesses of his syntax and the colourful limitations of his vocabulary.

'Just enough,' he thought, 'to impress the girls selling sweets and *la môme Cassart*. . . .'

For a fortnight he had been watching her, the creature whom like everyone else he called 'the crazy old woman', the tall septuagenarian who retained the figure of someone young but out of date, her back straight in her stiff corset and her shoulders like those of a Prussian officer. Her organdie hats, her *broderie anglaise* dresses and her long pink or orchid-coloured veils flew on the jetty like flags, and when schoolboys followed her they walked quickly in order to see her face, a death's head covered with make-up, spotted with globules of paraffin which had sunk down beneath the skin on her cheeks, over a neck tightly swathed in boned tulle.

He had noticed her at the famous confectioner's, clinking

all over with jewels, as pink as a piece of crackleware wax fruit; he had waited while she greedily took away a packet of special chocolate. After she had gone on her calm and scandalous way he bought some almond biscuits.

'To send to the Hôtel Beauséjour? For Monsieur. . . ?'

'Monsieur Paul Dagueret.'

'D apostrophe?'

He smiled casually at the blonde salesgirl.

'As you wish, Mademoiselle. It doesn't bother me.'

The blonde salesgirl, impressed by this aristocratic insouciance, allowed herself to make a few jokes about Madame Cassart, and deplored the fact that such diamonds . . .

'I didn't notice,' interrupted Monsieur Dagueret coldly. 'I'm not a connoisseur.'

Now, in *la môme Cassart*'s bedroom, he was searching not for the diamonds which she hardly ever took off, but for the compensation merited by his solitary and persevering work.

'Even if it's only a gold chain, or those big round bracelets that she puts over her old bones,' he murmured as he searched quietly through the light, commonplace room where Madame Cassart had revealed her personal taste by pinning up everywhere bows of ribbon and flowers made of coloured breadcrumbs. . . .

As he went through a drawer with his electric torch he rejected an aquamarine cross and took a gold locket worth at least fifty francs. At that precise moment he heard a musical squeak from the garden gate and then a key in the lock down below. Heavy steps could already be heard on the stairs when he decided to seek refuge behind the undrawn curtains at the French windows.

He immediately felt uncomfortable and frustrated. On

other days this crazy old woman had never returned home from the casino before midnight. Between the curtains he could see her going backwards and forwards and hear her muttering indistinctly. She no longer bothered to thrust her head back in military style and she walked with rounded shoulders, mouthing in senile fashion. As she carefully took off her youthful hat and drew out her hairpins the prisoner saw a pale little tonsure surrounded with hair that was still luxurious and dyed bright red. The *décolleté* dress came down, a beribboned *négligé* concealed the grained skin with its little red spots caused by the sea air, and the sinister dewlaps at the neck. Beneath the loose hair the angry face, made up as though for some drama, increased Monsieur Paul Dagueret's uneasiness.

'What can I do?' he wondered. 'Obviously I must do what's necessary, but. . . . A filly like that is quite something! Oh dear me. . . .'

He cared neither for noise nor bloodshed, and each second increased his discomfort. Madame Cassart spared him any further anguish. All at once she turned her head towards the curtains as though she had suddenly smelt him, pulled them apart, uttered a cry hardly louder than a sigh and recoiled three steps, hiding her face in her hands. He was just about to take advantage of this unexpected gesture and flee when she said to him, without uncovering her face, in an affected and suppliant voice: 'Why did you do it? Oh, why?'

He was standing between the parted curtains, bareheaded —a hat or a cap always gets lost—wearing his gloves, his hair ruffled. She went on, in the loud, crystalline voice typical of old people: 'You should never have done it!'

She lowered her hands and he saw to his stupefaction that

she was looking at him without fear, in a loving, submissive way.

'Here we go. A scene,' he thought.

'Did you have to be so impulsive?' sighed Madame Cassart. 'Couldn't you just have introduced yourself in a more conventional way? Did you imagine I hadn't noticed or guessed anything? It was quite easy for you to. . . . But not like this, oh, not like this!'

She drew herself up, put her hair back on top of her head and draped her wrap round her with the dignity of an elderly clown.

The man was disconcerted and remained silent, and then said in mechanical fashion : 'If ever anyone had . . .'

She interrupted him in a palpitating voice.

'No, no, don't say anything, you'll never know how upset I am . . . I am . . . my reputation is unimpeachable . . . I've never been married. . . . They call me Madame, but. . . . Your presence here. . . . Oh, can't you see how it upsets me. . . . You won't get anything from me this way, I can assure you!'

Every gesture she made, every sigh she uttered awoke the aggressive sparkle of her diamonds, but the burglar did not look at them any longer, he was preoccupied with the anger of a healthy and, moreover, modest man. He nearly exploded and told—and in what terms!—this impassioned old woman what to do with herself. He took one step and in front of him, in a mirror, he saw the flattering image of a handsome young man, dressed in black, and distinguished certainly. . . .

'Tell me that I'll see you again, but first, away from my house,' simpered the crazy woman. 'Give me your word as a gentleman!'

Distinguished, yes, when he kept silent. A kind of snobbery removed from him the desire to insult and brutalize, a snobbery which respected simultaneously the old woman's absurd mistake and the moment of his own life which simulated the life of a noble and romantic hero. He bowed as best he could and said in a deep voice : 'You have my word, Madame !'

And went away, speechless.

The Murderer

When he had killed her, with a blow from the little lead hammer under which she kept her wrapping-paper, Louis felt embarrassed. She lay behind the counter, with one leg bent sideways, her head turned away and her body facing forward, in a ridiculous posture which put the young man into a bad temper. He shrugged his shoulders and almost said to her : 'Get up then, you look very odd !' But at that moment the doorbell rang and Louis saw a little girl come in.

'A card of black mending wool, please,' she said.

'We haven't any more,' he answered politely, 'we shan't have any until tomorrow !'

She went out, closing the door carefully, and he noticed that he had not even thought that she might have come up to the counter, leant over, seen. . . .

Dusk was falling, making the little stationer's-cum-haberdasher's shop dark. It was still possible to see the rows of white boxes with ivory buttons or balls of braid on their sides. Louis struck a match mechanically on the sole of his shoe to light the gas jet, then he remembered, and extinguished the match with his foot. The wine merchant opposite suddenly lit up his ground floor and by contrast the little haberdasher's-cum-stationer's subsided into darkness streaked with rays of yellow light.

Once again Louis leant over the counter. With utter astonishment he realized that his mistress was still there, with her leg bent and her neck turned sideways. Moreover, something black, a thread as fine as a lock of hair, was trickling over the pale cheek. He picked up the forty-five francs in small change and the dirty notes that he had so furiously turned down earlier, went out, removed the key, put it in his pocket and went away.

For two days he lived in a kind of childhood state, amusing himself by watching the boats on the Seine and the schoolchildren in the squares. Like a child he was amused and like a child he was bored. He waited and could not decide to leave the town, nor to set himself up selling cheap goods as he had done before. His room, which he rented by the week, still contained, however, a stock of postcards showing the buildings of Paris, jumping rabbits and products in tubes for making fruit drinks. But Louis sold nothing for two days and went to sleep in another furnished room. He didn't feel afraid, and he slept well; the day passed easily for him, filled only with that pleasant impatience one feels in great ports after booking one's passage on a liner.

Two days after the crime he bought a paper, as on other days, and read : 'A woman shopkeeper murdered in rue X. . .' 'Aha,' he said aloud like a connoisseur, read the news-item slowly and attentively, noted that the crime, due to the 'very retired' existence led by the victim, was already regarded as 'mysterious', and folded the paper. His *café crème* was going cold in front of him. The bar waiter was whistling as he polished the zinc, an old couple beside him were dipping croissants into warm milk. Louis remained stupefied for a moment or so, and with his mouth half open he wondered why these familiar things had suddenly ceased to be near and intelligible. He had the impression that if he were to question the old couple they would reply in a strange language, and that the waiter, as he whistled, was looking through Louis's body without being aware of his presence.

He stood up, threw down his money and started out towards a small station, where he took a ticket for a suburb whose name reminded him of races and afternoons in a canoe. During the journey he felt that the train was making very little noise and that the travellers were talking in subdued voices.

'Perhaps I'm going deaf?'

As he left the train, Louis bought an evening paper, read the same story as in the morning paper and yawned.

'Good heavens, it hasn't got any further!'

He ate in a little restaurant near the station and asked the proprietor about the possibility of finding work in the district. But he carried out this formality with great repugnance, and felt uneasy when the restaurant-owner advised him to see a dentist living in a nearby villa; he had unfortunately just lost a young man who had been employed, up till the day before, to clean his motor-cycle and sterilize his instruments. In spite of the late hour he rang the dentist's doorbell, said he was a manufacturer of mechanical toys, did not argue about the rate of pay—two hundred and fifty francs—and slept that same night in a little attic room papered with the grey and blue flower-patterned paper that is used for lining cheap trunks.

For a week he kept the job of laboratory assistant to the American dentist, a tall, horselike man with prominent bones and red hair, who asked him no questions and smoked with his feet on the table while waiting for his rare clients. Wearing a white linen smock Louis would lean against the open gate to breathe in the fresh air, and the maids from the villas would smile as they looked at his brown, gentle face.

Every day he bought a paper. The 'crime in rue X' had been banished from the front page and now languished on the second page, among train crashes and thefts committed by somnambulists. Five or ten lines confirmed without excitement that 'the mystery remained complete'.

On a spring afternoon, perfumed by a brief shower of rain and pierced with the cries of swallows, Louis asked the American dentist for a little money 'to buy himself some underwear', took off his white smock and left again for Paris. And since he was just a simple little murderer he went straight to the stationer's-cum-haberdasher's. Children were playing outside the lowered iron shutter and the door was covered with a week's splashes of mud. Louis walked up and down the pavement opposite and did not leave the street until after nightfall.

He came back the next day a little later, in order not to attract attention, and every evening afterwards he faithfully did his sentry-go after dinner, sometimes without dinner. He felt full of a strange hope, resembling the anguish of love. One evening when he had stopped in order to look up at the stars and sigh deeply, a hand was placed lightly on his shoulder. He closed his eyes, did not look round, then fell limply and happily into the arms of the policeman who was following him.

During his interrogation Louis admitted that he certainly regretted his crime, but that a moment like the one when he felt the liberating hand on his shoulder 'made up for everything', and that he could only compare it to the one when he had, he said, 'known love'.

Growing old in good health with quiet little
refully prepared little meals. . . .
think it's better than hanging about in dance-
rooms and casinos?' Lily would say.
nod in agreement, adding : 'Everything's so
r a memory like that. . . .'

*

cupboard was tidy Alice changed her dress,
white leather belt round her waist and smiled :
ole as last year! It's really quite amusing!'
reproached herself for being late in greeting, in
floor drawing-room, 'their' portrait. . . .
Alice! Are you coming down?'
calling her from below : she leant down over the
lustrade : 'Just a minute! What is it?'
own. . . . It's something odd. . . . Come on!'
upset, always ready for some romantic encounter,
own and found Lily in front of 'their' portrait,
had taken down and stood on an armchair in the

months, in the darkness of the closed-up villa, the
dampness, some combination of salt and colour, had
a subtle disaster, a work of destruction in which
had acted with a near-miraculous malevolence. On
t man's Roman-looking chin, mould had created the
beard of an unkempt old man. The paper had
creating two lymphatic pouches above his cheeks.
grains of charcoal, slipping down from the hair over
ole portrait, loaded the conqueror's face with years
rinkles. . . . Alice put her white hands over her eyes :
. . it's vandalism!'

The Portrait

They opened the windows in their communicating bedrooms
at the same time, rattled down the Venetian blinds which
were half closed against the sun, and smiled at each other as
they leant against the wooden balcony.

'What weather!'

'Not a wrinkle on the sea!'

'Lucky sea! Did you notice how much the wistaria's
grown since last year?'

'And the honeysuckle! The shoots have got caught in the
blinds now.'

'Are you going to rest, Lily?'

'I'm going to get a pullover and go down, I assure you! I
can't keep still the first day. What are you going to do,
Alice?'

'I'm going to sort out my linen cupboard. It smells of last
year's lavender. Let me do it. I find it madly entertaining.
You just do what you want.'

Lily tossed her short peroxided hair in a Guignol-like
gesture and a moment later Alice saw her, dressed in apple-
green, go down into the sandy garden, which was exposed to
the sea-breeze.

Alice laughed, not unkindly.

'How plump she is!'

She looked down with satisfaction at her own long white
hands and folded her thin forearms over the wooden rail,
breathing in the salt and iodine that enriched the air. The
breeze did not disturb a single hair of her Spanish-style

coiffure, in which the hair was smoothed back, baring the forehead and ears, flattering to her attractive, well-shaped nose, but not to all those things about her that were deteriorating: horizontal wrinkles above her eyebrows, sunken cheeks and eyes black-ringed through insomnia.

Her friend Lily attacked the severe hair-style: 'What can I say? Personally I think that when fruit gets rather dry it needs some leaves!'

To which Alice replied: 'Not everyone, when they're forty, can do their hair like a young thing from the Folies!'

They lived together in perfect harmony, and every day this teasing added fuel to the flames of their friendship. Alice, who was elegant and bony, would cheerfully say: 'My weight hasn't really changed since the year my husband died. And I've kept one of the blouses I wore as a girl, just out of curiosity: you'd think it had been made for me yesterday!'

Lily made no mention, and for good reason, of any marriage. The forties, after a wild youth, had endowed her with an incurable *embonpoint*.

'It's true I'm chubby,' she would declare. 'But look at my face: not one wrinkle! And the same's true of the rest! That's quite something, you must admit!'

And she would cast a malicious glance at Alice's hollow cheeks, at the scarf or the fox fur destined to hide the tendons in the neck or the protruding collar-bones. . . .

But love, more than rivalry, linked these two friends together: the same man, handsome, famous long before he grew old, had turned them both down. In the case of Alice, a few letters from the great man proved that for a few weeks he had taken a fancy to the slender brunette, her jealous eyes, her fateful, skilfully veiled elegance. Lily had kept nothing she had received from him except one telegram,

strangely laconic a
both of them, and
uttered by the two fi
almost sincere, and t

'I never understoo
'But there was a mon
have been a true frien
man, nobody has been

'As to that, my dear,
'True friend, guide . .
words. I do know that be
ness! things were hot! V
can assure you! I felt, ju
that I could have domin
then it broke up. . . . It alv

They were satisfied in fac
having reached the age whe
they had hung up in the dra
they lived together, sharing e
trait of the great man, the be
the daily papers and the illus
photograph, retouched, weig
patches like a violent etching,
on the mouth and blue on the e

'It's not exactly a work of a
someone who knew him as I d
alive!'

For two years they had resign
religious solitude, entertaining fr
and long-standing, well-worn men
my goodness, one must get used to
watched by that young portrait, l

memory. . . .
expeditions, ca
'Don't you
halls, massage
Alice woul
ordinary, aft

When the
fastened a v
The same
But she
the ground
'Alice! A
Lily was
wooden ba
'Come
Vaguel
she ran
which sh
light.
In ten
unusual
contrive
chance
the grea
whitish
swollen
A few
the wh
and w
'It's .

The prosaic Lily sighed expressively : 'Well, now !' Then she added, feverishly : 'We're not going to leave him there, are we?'

'Good heavens no ! I couldn't bear it !'

They looked at each other. Lily found Alice youthful in her slenderness, and Alice could not restrain a feeling of envy : 'What a lovely complexion Lily has ! Like a peach !'

At lunch there was plenty of unusual chat, about massages, diets, dresses and the nearby casino. They spoke as though incidentally about the extended youth of certain artistes and their publicized love-affairs. Without any apparent motive Lily cried 'A life that's short and sweet? I'd rather have it long and gay !' Alice mentioned in an absent-minded way, four or five times, the name of a man, one of their friends who was due—'or I'm very much mistaken'—to spend the summer in the district. . . . A feverish wish to escape, a warm flood of unsatisfactory plans, made them eat and drink a lot, smoke cigarettes and talk freely. But in the drawing-room Alice turned her face away pityingly as she passed in front of the portrait and it was the vulgar Lily, red-faced and slightly tipsy, who disdainfully blew smoke at the great man's face : 'Poor old thing ! . . .'

The Landscape

The painter who wanted to die made the gesture, at once spontaneous and literary, of writing a few lines before killing himself. He pulled towards him a large sheet of drawing-paper and a pencil and then, just as he was about to write, he had second thoughts.

'A few lines? For whom? The concierge knows I live alone, that I've no family, that my mistress has left me. . . . Let's give her the pleasure of recounting this unimportant accident once to the commissioner of police and twenty times to the neighbours. My canvases? They can be sold. I'd cheerfully burn them, but how exhausting. . . . And the smell of burning oil and charred hemp, in this fine weather. . . . Pah, I don't want my last earthly memory to be a sickening smell.'

Yet he hesitated, tormented by a childish feeling of restlessness, a kind of vanity and truly vital integrity : the need to leave behind him some trace of his passing and note the hour of his disappearance, a need equivalent in fact to that of recounting his wretched life as a betrayed lover. . . . He threw down the pencil.

'People will think I'm trying to gain pity after I'm dead. Die then, without any fuss ! Is it so difficult to die simply?'

He seized his revolver, loaded it and his right arm instinctively sought the ready support of his big armchair; facing him, a virgin canvas on the easel reflected back on to his face the sweet yellow light of the spring afternoon. He put the weapon down on a small table and rose slowly.

'Yes . . . that's something I can do. I must do it, really. I see within me this landscape which resembles my life, which explains why I'm dying. . . .'

He began to paint, rapidly, with broad, free strokes which were not characteristic of him. He barely stopped to contemplate within himself his model, the landscape composed of his stormy, youthful grief, sometimes sharply outlined, sometimes scattered with clouds which passed only to restore its blinding clarity and somewhat conventional symbolism.

He painted a marshy plain, a kind of desert in the Sologne, where the greenish-black reeds stood in isolated groups in leaden-coloured pools of water. From the foreground, where a few hollow leaves floated like skiffs, to the horizon sealed with a rigid bar of cirrus, there were only reedy marshes, flat desolation, reflections wrinkled by the wind of a sky where the parallel banks of low cloud moved forward like the swell of the sea.

In the foreground a single bare tree stood bent beneath the storm just as grasses in a river follow the current. The main branch, broken yet living, revealed the splintered white sapwood beneath its torn bark. . . .

The impetuous hand finally stopped, the arm grew stiff and fell alongside the body. A warm fatigue softened this last hour of life.

'That's good,' the painter said to himself. 'My portrait resembles me. I'm pleased. Now there's nothing to keep me any longer. I'm going to die.'

The rectangular patch of sky above the bay window changed from yellow to pink, heralding a long springtime twilight. A young woman's voice, quite near, sang through the open window the first notes of a song so piercing, so colourful, that the painter, holding his breath, looked at the window as though he expected to see the sounds pass by in the shape of copper balls, round-petalled flowers, fruit moist with juice. Holding the revolver in his hand he leant down with curiosity into the courtyard. He did not discover there the young singer whose mouth was sending such a generous farewell towards his death. But on the other side of the courtyard, in a gloomy little apartment, a girl's fair hair shone like a truss of straw in a dark hayloft.

The painter returned to his canvas, sat down and felt the armchair with his right arm. . . . At the sound of a prolonged B flat a fragile crystal glass close to him vibrated.

'There's something missing from this picture. . . . A link . . . some intelligible detail. . . . A detail which would be like the humble caption of the picture. . . .'

He put his revolver down and began to paint, on the main branch of the tree, a grey bird, a singing bird, swelling with music, its head raised singing to the cloudy sky.

The painter was pleased with the lustre of the plumage, the glow of the eye, like a black jet bead. . . . When evening fell and a servant came up, bringing his meal, she found the painter standing in front of his canvas, beside a weapon that had been forgotten. He had used the last lilac-coloured rays of sunlight to sketch in at the foot of the bare tree a flower, which was still unfinished, its sickly, obstinate petal-face rising out of the marsh.

Secrets

'It's not an engagement party, no. . . . But nobody's taken in. Tomorrow I'll be forced to announce to everyone that Claudie Grey is engaged to André Donat, otherwise I'll have a scandal on my hands. The child hasn't danced with anyone except him and all our friends are on their side. Even Charles. . . .'

Madame Grey looked for her husband and saw him seated at a poker table. 'Well now, he's still running his thumb-nail over his lip. Again . . . again . . . and again. . . . Last week I didn't surprise him at it once. It's this tiring weather, with the storm that won't break. . . .' She sighed, and her gaze settled on her daughter and André Donat who were dancing to the sound of the pianola. Claudie resembled her, she was just as tall, and just as fair as she had been at the same age.

'Fair . . . not for long. That type of fairness goes white quickly, I ought to know. But the child looks very nice this evening. Really very nice. Just like her mother. As for her face, the likeness is disconcerting, in spite of the way the features seem smaller. Smaller nose, smaller eyes unfortunately, a smaller mouth than I have, thank goodness. . . . She looks very nice. I can put my name to her, as they say. And a good girl. . . . Oh, I really feel it's all over and she's going to leave me! I'm singing her praises as though. . . .'

She brought her train of thought to an abrupt end and superstitiously touched a wooden gilt chair. For her only daughter Madame Grey had a professional tenderness that was incapable of blindness, the kind of critical devotion which binds the trainer to the champion. Her own health, her mental and physical equilibrium, had often made her uncompromising and severe on the subject of feminine weaknesses that she did not share.

'What, migraine? You've got migraine? And where would you have unearthed a migraine, I never knew what it was ! . . . A chignon low down? You want to wear a chignon low down? Silly little thing, when I was your age nothing suited me less. . . . What you need is the helmet style, and you must leave the back of your neck uncovered : look at the portrait Ferdinand Humbert painted of me !'

In her daughter Madame Grey cherished a little girl of 1885, in a short dress, her legs bare and washed in cold water; a young girl of 1895, riding in the Bois, her hair in a catogan beneath the black bowler; a 'good child', easy to bring up, somewhat on the bold side, as clean-cut as a pedigree filly, a tall lanky girl who had never heard of hysteria and wouldn't call out three doctors when her first baby was born.

Madame Grey looked at her future son-in-law with the vindictive eyes of a mother-in-law.

'Yes, everyone thinks him a good-looking boy. And everything on a plate, he'll take over his father's business. Envy, this marriage will cause nothing but envy. And if I said what I really thought about it, there'd be a real outcry ! . . .'

André Donat, as he left the tango to go to the buffet for a moment, bowed as he passed in front of Madame Grey, kissed her hand lightly, took the little handkerchief from her wrist and fled, laughing and showing his white teeth. Madame Grey threatened him with her fan and smiled at him without kindness. She reached the terrace, sat down and breathed in the dusty coolness of the Bois at night. Her fifty inflexible years sagged a little in the solitude, her knees felt stiff, and her proud back demanded her bed, the well-smoothed cambric, the soft rubber hot-water bottle, scorching hot. . . .

'That boy's putting on a show of being nice to me. For how long? . . . When he laughs he shows protruding canine teeth in his upper jaw, and little incisors below, too short and looking as if they've been filed down; coarseness, quick sexual reactions . . . I'm sorry for my daughter if she has pretty chambermaids. . . . That nose is too short, it shows a lack of judgment. . . . And his ear-lobes are joined to the back of his cheeks : that's degeneracy. . . . And when we paid him a visit at his home, he was proud of the fact that he couldn't live in chaos, that he arranged books by the colour of their covers, and got up in the night to put trees in his shoes. . . .'

Madame Grey shuddered and stood up. She saw with the eye of memory a young woman, utterly overwhelmed, faced by a young man in his shirt, standing barefoot on a mosaic bathroom floor, a young man confessing, with horrible unconscious frankness, that if the fringes of the Turkish towels on the towel-rail did not all hang level he couldn't sleep : 'It's odd, darling, I'm quite Bohemian in other ways, but the fringes on the Turkish towels. . . .'

'But I can't tell Claudie that,' thought Madame Grey, in a state of agitation. 'No. I can't. If I tell her that, and that I nearly left her father because of the way he runs his thumb-nail over his lip, she'll laugh. She won't understand. And these are things you don't speak about. The night before a girl gets married, you can whisper a few things in her ear, you're shy, and clumsy. . . . But I could never talk to her about the fringes of the towels, nor about the thumb-nail running over the lip a hundred times, nor. . . . Oh, that'll do! She'll hide things from me . . . little, terrible things, the mould that grows on married life, the rubbish that a man's character throws away at the boundary of childishness and madness. . . .

'My poor child. . . .' Madame Grey sighed, drew herself up, her tall figure revealing how she had lost in suppleness and gained in majesty, and returned to the drawing-room. She made only a brief sign to the engaged couple who were dancing a Boston two-step and hurried towards the poker table.

'Make room for me, Charles. There are only four of you. . . .'

She had no wish to play poker. But she sat down next to her husband and with a meaningful grip she restrained the hand which unconsciously passed and repassed over the lip a hundred times and a hundred times more. . . .

'Châ'

His wife placed her hand on his shoulder as she went by :
'Are you glad you're going to see the little dolls dance?'

He didn't much care for this trite way of describing the
Cambodian dancers, but he nodded assent and admired his
wife as she moved away. She was wearing a silver dress, with
sulphur-coloured roses at her waist, and carrying a large
fan of sulphur-coloured feathers, while her hair, skilfully
bleached to a very pale gold, looked like a head-dress bought
at the same time as the roses and the fan. She was tall, and
impressed others through the somewhat rudimentary beauty
of her features and her virile blue eyes, which were accustomed to judging everything from above.

'The beautiful Madame Issard is superb this evening,'
said a man's voice from behind a white silk curtain painted
with beige bamboo.

'Combat dress,' replied another voice. 'It's this evening
that she hopes to arrange with the Marshal that her husband
can have the mission.'

'It's hardly right for Issard, that mission. He's a man of
letters . . . subtle and stay-at-home . . .'

'But it's right for Madame Issard. In four months she'll
carry off the rosette for Issard and perhaps the ribbon for
herself. Did you hear her at table? It was magnificent. What
diplomacy! And at the same time it's irreproachable . . . I
don't feel sorry for Issard.'

André Issard left the bamboo-painted curtain. Not that
he was afraid of hearing anything about his wife that might

73

have made him angry. But he felt the need to have a short rest from the long admiration shown to his wife during dinner. Moreover, the Cambodian girls were preceded by kettledrums, each one emitting on its own the liquid note which can be heard in the throats of toads; the girls were beginning their dance on a platform in front of Pierre Guesde's fifty guests, who were scattered throughout the hall. Issard, with a blasé expression behind his monocle, took great pleasure in seeing them. His ideas of exoticism did not go beyond Algiers, and he had only seen Ith, Sarrouth, Trassoth and their companions in *L'Illustration*. He found them pretty, while regretting that their round cheeks were painted with white lead. He disapproved of the fashion, originating in Siam, which endowed them with a hair-style like that of small boys. But even if they had heads like boys, most of them had necks like the shafts of columns, without creases or blemishes, and their skin was smooth, taut, the colour of fine stoneware, sometimes the colour of little plums, ravishing to look at. André Issard sought for words which were not too overworked to describe these inscrutable children's faces which had been carved entirely on the surface— eyes slit with lightweight scissors, the nose barely emerging from the cheek, the mouth whose short little lips revealed the soft red interior. . . . With the obstinacy of an artistic scribbler he wondered how he would paint the curve of Sarrouth's hands, and the fingers bent back to prolong a palm that curved inwards. . . .

'A leaf burnt up by autumn? No. . . . Rather the twisting of a fish when it's out of the water. . . . Or else. . . . Yes, that's it : it's the heraldic curl in the tongue of a breathless dog. . . .'

Then the music and the magic of the movements acted together and André Issard hardly thought of anything else.

'They're pretty . . . they're new . . . they're . . . they're feminine, very feminine. . . .'

He looked up and caught sight of his wife in a deep alcove; she was not watching the dancing but talking to the governor of a large colony. She spoke, listened, spoke again and seemed to use as much energy in listening as in speaking. Her brows met heavily over her blue eyes, their gaze contemplating a glorious and austere future.

'She looks like a man,' André Issard said to himself. 'Why hadn't I noticed it before?'

At the same moment the beautiful Madame Issard rested her chin on her hands and faced everyone present, her attention apparently acquiring powerful supporters in one place after another. Then she went on with the conversation, very quietly, and André Issard noticed how she moved her chin up and down like a democratic leader, how her clenched fist tapped out the rhythm of her sentence.

'She's a man,' Issard repeated to himself. 'I wondered, unfairly, what I had against her. . . . The fact is that my wife's a man . . . and what a man! . . . I've only got what I deserve; I should have realized it sooner!'

The dance was coming to an end. In a fatalistic way he moved towards the platform where the little dancers had scattered and were being subjected, at close quarters, to the wounding curiosity of the Europeans. He listened to Pierre Guesde talking in Cambodian with Soun, a singer from the choir, who wasn't made up but scintillated with black eyes and white teeth; he allowed himself to be introduced to Ith, who was dressed as a Burmese prince, Ith with the innocent face made famous through a hundred photographs; he touched Sarrouth's hands, melting, moving hands. . . . While Sarrouth listened to Pierre Guesde, André Issard held them

in his own, those hands as passive and cool as leaves covered
with flesh. She replied with a brief murmur, a little deferen-
tial greeting, a childish laugh, and above all with a mono-
syllable, '*Châ . . . Châ . . .*'

'*Tia . . .*' repeated Issard, imitating Sarrouth's liquid pro-
nunciation. 'What does that mean?'

'It means,' explained Pierre Guesde, 'very-respectfully-
yes.'

The dancers were leaving, and Issard motioned to his wife,
'Are we going home?' She replied in the same way with a
furious and barely visible 'no'. Ten minutes later he noticed,
close to him, her scent and the scalelike swish of her dress.

'The Marshal's leaving,' she said to him.

He leapt up.

'I'll dash over!' . . .

'No,' she said. 'Leave it. I've arranged a personal inter-
view for you tomorrow.'

'The least I can do is to . . .'

'No,' she said. 'Leave it, I tell you. You can take it from
me. Everything's all right. I've sown a seed, and sown it well.'

She shone with a mineral-like glow, and took him towards
the exit. In the car she called out to the chauffeur, 'Go back
past the Prado!' and placed her arm under her husband's,
with a kind of condescending cordiality, the good humour of
a despotic woman. The full moon covered her pale hair with
powdery silver, and the great sulphur-yellow feathers in her
fan rolled like waves in the wind. But André Issard did not
see her. He was humming a little song imitating Asiatic
music, and stopped in order to murmur under his breath,
'*Châ . . . Châ . . .*'

'What did you say, André dear?'

He smiled at his wife, with the look of a disloyal slave:
'Oh, nothing. . . . It's a Cambodian word, more or less un-
translatable. . . . A word that has no meaning here. . . .'

The Bracelet

' . . . Twenty-seven, twenty-eight, twenty-nine. . . . There really are twenty-nine. . . .'

In mechanical fashion Madame Angelier counted and re-counted the little rows of diamonds. Twenty-nine brilliant, square diamonds, set in a bracelet, sliding coldly like a thin, supple snake between her fingers. Very white, not very big, admirably well matched—a real connoisseur's piece. She fastened it round her wrist and made it sparkle under the electric candles; a hundred tiny rainbows, ablaze with colour, danced on the white table-cloth. But Madame Angelier looked more closely at the other bracelet, three finely engraved wrinkles which encircled her wrist above the brilliant snake.

'Poor François. . . . If we're both still here, what will he give me next year?'

François Angelier was a businessman travelling in Algeria at the time but, present or absent, his gift marked the end of the year and the anniversary of their wedding. Twenty-eight pieces of green jade, last year; the year before, twenty-seven plaques of old enamel mounted on a belt. . . .

'And the twenty-six little Dresden plates. . . . And the twenty-five metres of old Alençon lace. . . .' With a slight effort of memory Madame Angelier could have gone as far back as the four modest sets of knives and forks, the three pairs of silk stockings. . . .

'We weren't rich, just then. . . . Poor François, how he has always spoiled me. . . .' She called him, within her secret self, 'poor François', because she felt guilty about not loving him enough, failing to appreciate the power of affectionate habit and enduring fidelity.

Madame Angelier raised her hand, crooked her little finger upwards, extended her wrist in order to erase the bracelet of wrinkles, and repeated with concentration, 'How pretty it is. . . . How clear the diamonds are. . . . How pleased I am. . . .' Then she let fall her hand and admitted that she was already tired of the brand-new piece of jewellery.

'But I'm not ungrateful,' she sighed naïvely. Her bored glance wandered from the flowered table-cloth to the sparkling window. The smell of Calville apples in a silver basket made her feel slightly sick and she left the dining-room.

In her boudoir she opened the steel case which contained her jewellery and decked out her left hand in honour of the new bracelet. The ring finger had a ring of black onyx, a brilliant tinged with blue; over the little finger, which was delicate, pale and slightly wrinkled, Madame Angelier slipped a hoop of dark sapphires. Her prematurely white hair, which she did not dye, looked whiter when she fixed into its light curls a narrow little band sprinkled with a dust of diamonds, but she removed the ornament at once.

'I don't know what's the matter with me. I'm not in form. It's tedious being fifty, in fact. . . .'

She felt uneasy, greedy, but not hungry, like a convalescent whose appetite has not yet been restored by the fresh air.

'Actually, is a diamond as pretty as all that?'

Madame Angelier yearned for visual pleasure combined with the pleasure of taste; the unexpected sight of a lemon, the unbearable squeak of the knife which cuts it in two, makes one's mouth water with desire. . . .

'I don't want a lemon. But the nameless pleasure which

escapes me, it exists, I know it, I remember it! So, the blue glass bracelet. . . .'

A shudder contracted Madame Angelier's relaxed cheeks. A miracle, the duration of which she could not measure, allowed her, for the second time, the moment she had lived through forty years earlier, the incomparable moment when she looked in rapture at the light of day, the rainbow-coloured and misshapen image of objects through a piece of blue glass, bent into a circle, which had just been given to her. That piece of glass, which might have come from the East and was broken a few hours later, had contained a new universe, shapes that dreaming did not invent, slow, serpentine animals which moved in pairs, lamps, rays congealed in an atmosphere of indescribable blue . . .

The miracle ended and Madame Angelier, feeling bruised, was thrown back into the present and the real.

But from the next day she went from antique dealers to bargain basements, from bargain basements to glassware shops, looking for a glass bracelet of a certain blue. She did so with the passion of a collector, the care and dissimulation of a crank. She ventured into what she called 'impossible districts', left her car at the corner of strange streets and in the end, for a few centimes, found a hoop of blue glass that she recognized in the darkness, bought mutteringly and took away. . . .

By the suitably adjusted shade of her favourite lamp, on the dark background of old velvet, she put down the bracelet, bent over it, awaited the shock. . . . But she saw only a circle of bluish glass, an ornament for a child or a savage, moulded hastily, full of bubbles; an object whose colour and material she recalled; but the powerful and sensuous genie who creates and feeds the visions of childhood, who dies mysteriously within us, progressively disappearing, did not stir.

With resignation Madame Angelier realized in this way her true age and measured the infinite plain over which there moved a being forever detached from herself, inaccessible, foreign, turning away from her, free and rebellious even to the command of memory : a little girl of ten wearing round her wrist a bracelet of blue glass.

The Find

The light from the setting sun touched the curtains, shone through the drawing-room from end to end, and Irène's friends cried out in admiration.

'It's like fairyland!'

'And the Seine's on fire!'

'The sky's going pink . . .'

One of them was more honest, as she took in with one glance the Seine, the old drawing-room extended by a rustic dining-room, the purple and silver curtains, the orange tea-cups and the wood-fire.

'There's no justice in the world,' she murmured vindictively.

And poor little Madame Auroux, who had got divorced in order to marry and couldn't marry because she couldn't find an apartment, had two such heartfelt tears in her blue eyes that Irène put her arms round her tightly.

'She's in such a hurry to do something silly all over again! My pet, I believe that getting divorced brought me luck. For it must be said that finding this wonderful place was a stroke of luck. . . .'

She felt triumph without any shame and showed off her lovely home, although she would never have dared flash a new ring in front of an impoverished friend. She stretched herself.

'Children, children,' she admitted, as though she were making some guilty confession, 'if you knew what it's like here in the mornings! Those boats, and the reflection of the water dancing on the ceiling. . . .'

But they couldn't bear it any longer. Green with envy and, moreover, surfeited with cakes, they all left together. Leaning on the wrought-iron balustrade—'an eighteenth-century gem, my dear!'—Irène called out to them 'goodbye, goodbye', waving her hand as people do from the steps of a country château. She went back inside and leant her forehead against the window-pane. A brief winter twilight rapidly extinguished the pink and gold reflection of the sky in the water, and the first star flickered slowly, announcing a frosty night.

Irène heard a tinkling behind her as the cups were collected too quickly, and the rapid steps of her servant. She turned round.

'Are you in a hurry, Pauline?'

'I'm not exactly in a hurry, Madame, but I have my husband. . . . It's Saturday, and Madame knows they have a five-day week.'

'All right, all right. . . . You can do the washing-up tomorrow. No, don't lay the table for me, I've eaten so much tea, I certainly won't be hungry this evening.'

Since moving in she had put up with sketchy dinners, or cold meat from the nearby delicatessen, because of Pauline, a general maid who slept out. Some evenings when she was very energetic Irène would don a blue apron, grill raw ham herself and crack two eggs into a buttered dish. . . .

She heard the door bang hard and Pauline's clogs on the staircase. A tram sang on its rails along the quay opposite. The house was solid and old and hardly shook as cars went by, and its thick walls did not let through either the barking of the dog next door or the piano from the floor above.

Irène placed another log on the fire and near the fireplace—
'period shell marble, my dear !'—she arranged the little desk-
table, the big armchair, the books, the screen, and remained
standing, contemplating the background to her happiness.
. . . A clock outside struck slowly.

'Seven o'clock. Only seven o'clock. Still thirteen hours
until tomorrow. . . .'

She shuddered humbly; in front of the unresponsive wit-
nesses—the purple curtains, the building which stood out
against the night sky like the prow of a liner, the useless
armchair and the book that had lost its magic—she abdicated
from her state of being a happy woman, a woman of whom
people say 'she has no worries' and 'a unique apartment'.

No more tiresome and destructive husband, no more
scenes, no more unexpected returns, departures that seemed
to be flights, suspect telegrams, invisible women on the telephone who were called 'old chap' or 'my dear sir'.

No more husband, no more child, admirers and no
lover. . . . 'Liberty on the mountain !' some of her jealous
friends would say.

'But did I ask for liberty on the mountain?'

She had taken back her dowry, recovered her indepen-
dence, moved into an old luxurious building, sunny and
secret, made for a recluse or a couple passionately in love,
and lived in peace—oh, what peace. . . .

'But did I need so much peace?'

She remained standing, in front of the armchair and the
screen which attempted, beneath the over-lofty ceiling, to
enclose round Irène a refuge of suitable size. She felt a
sudden need for light, lit the little chandelier of smoked
crystal with arms of antique bronze and the electric basket
of fruit on the dining-room table. But she left in darkness the

bedroom on which she had prided herself earlier, and her Spanish bed where four flames of gilded wood at the four corners rose like heraldic pales.

'My place is very attractive,' she decided, coldly. 'I've only to wait till it's time to show it to other women friends. And then what?'

She saw a series of days in which, acting as guide, she would praise the shell marble chimney-piece, the wrought-iron balustrade, the Seine, the woodwork with its faded gilt. . . . All at once, with a desperate ferocity, she envied a little furnished flat where for want of anything better a friend of hers lived with a young painter, two rooms messy with cigarette-ash and blobs of paint, but warm with quarrels, laughter, reconciliations. She felt at the same time a near-physical yearning, full of bitterness, for a studio which would serve as an apartment—one has to live somewhere!—for a whole family, the two parents, the three beautiful children who were as much alike as three pure-bred puppies. The warmth of the small, pleasure-loving apartment, the high vertical light from the studio window over the three naked little bodies. . . . Irène switched off the electricity suddenly, and sighed, slightly comforted, when the beautiful, antique order of the apartment disappeared. She moved the screen and the armchair away from the fire, drew the curtains, put on an old warm coat, switched out the last lamp in the drawing-room in a cautious and hostile manner and went out, taking a detective story, the caviar sandwiches and the chocolate-pot, to end her evening in a cane armchair squeezed in between the wash-basin and shower in the bathroom.

Mirror-Play

I don't enjoy it here, but it's so cold outside. . . . Here, as soon as you come in, the air surrounds you like an eiderdown. When I was a child I used to sleep in winter beneath a thick cloud of delicate goose-down imprisoned in red marceline, a choice, lightweight down which radiated a mysterious heat. Here it's just stuffy. You breathe in all the smells of a *salon de thé* : marzipan, crisp pastry, the vegetable bitterness of stewed tea, the rum in the *babas*, the scorched crumbs of a piece of toast that has fallen into the embers, and most of all perfumes, women's perfumes. . . . There are no sanctions against certain perfumers, the manufacture of scents is dangerously unrestricted, the feminine sense of smell, often rudimentary and badly educated, encounters and tries out everything that is sold in little bottles. The faded lavender of angelica, the waxy rose of geranium, extract of vanilla unnecessarily braced with resin, tarry narcissus, prussic acid lilac, creosoted carnation, benjamin disguised as amber, and all that vague flora, those distilled flower-beds revealing the inevitable, barely concealed, nauseous soul of wild parsnip.

I try to forget the scents that float about in cacophonous fashion. Moreover, the two women next to me are pretty and smell nice. The sandalwood worn by the brunette would tire me in the long run, and I know that behind the 'red rose' with which the blonde has sprayed herself there lies concealed, on the secondary, olfactory level, a vaguely fetid smell of fresh ink. But this brunette, this blonde and I are not going to spend our lives together.

The brunette is pretty and the peroxided blonde delightful. The brunette is resplendent, dressed entirely in grey velvet with panels of flame-coloured beads, silver fox furs round her neck, wearing shoes with sequins, feathers and strass, embroidered, funnel-shaped gloves, and a hat like a cloud of aigrettes, hanging like a threatened storm over two stars; she is resplendent with that slightly crude elegance that people like today. . . . The greedy and talkative women fell silent when she came in. They look at her, and the envious looks enhance her just as summer rain polishes the enamel on a kingfisher. She's warm, drinks like a pigeon with her neck extended and her jabot hanging forward. She has two gestures, frequent as tics, but they arise from a studied coquetry; with her first finger she pushes back a feather-light brown curl from one eyebrow and you see her almond-shaped nail gleam close to her elongated eye; at the nape of her neck she plunges a tortoise-shell trident into her hair and, when she raises her arm, one's eye follows the roundness of her well-supported breast which moves upwards along with her arm.

The blonde . . . the blonde is delightful in her own way. She's only a blonde in black marocain *crêpe* and a plush cape, a blonde with a short neck and a carnivorous mouth. Her tics don't beautify her. She thrusts her chin forward like a pug-dog and she wrinkles her nose like a little seal emerging from the water, blinking her eyes. It's not pretty. . . . I'd like to tell her so. . . . Good! Now, as everyone looks at her, she imitates her friend's behaviour. She thrusts out her bosom and taps her low golden chignon with one hand. Just as a younger sister unconsciously imitates an elder sister who already knows she is attractive. What pleasure these two well-bred peacocks give to the eyes! The more beautiful despises the more docile one slightly and the latter, not without a jealous shudder, imitates her, adapts herself, corrects herself. . . .

A man appears. Were they expecting him? I think so. For they both cried 'Well!' in tones of surprise. Which one did he come for? I don't know. One fills his cup, the other offers cakes. Impartial and courteous, he leans towards the blonde, then gives all his attention to what the brunette is saying. The blonde seems to be getting irritable, she thrusts her chin forward jerkily, wrinkles up her nose and laughs too much. Now she looks ugly beside her rival. . . . The man has eyes only for the brunette, with her dress of ash and flame, her white face, her pink forefinger, her round breast which reveals an independent strength beneath the dress. I'm putting my money on the brunette and I'm losing. The man turns imperceptibly, unconsciously, towards the blonde. At first his body turned slowly. The chair too, with little impatient gliding movements. The blonde can thrust her chin forward, repeat that common gesture which shortens her neck, wrinkle up her nose and show too much of her gums above her irregular teeth, she's no longer risking anything, the man prefers her. She triumphs and within a few moments takes on colour like a fruit touched by a ray of autumn.

And the brunette, agitated and uncertain, intervenes, tries to discover the secret of the victorious blonde and risks, in imitation, wrinkling her nose, blinking her eyes and making faces like a pug-dog, her jaw thrust forward and her teeth bared. . . .

Habit

They broke up in the same way as they had become close, without knowing why. It can, however, be taken for certain that Jeannine revealed to third parties, with too much explosive gaiety, that Andrée's real name, bestowed at her christening by one of her grandmothers, was Symphorienne. Another version asserted that Andrée clumsily overestimated her authority as the elder, and as a well-built brunette, and one afternoon, in front of twenty cups of tea and as many glasses of port, she gave her the signal to go, whistling for her as she whistled for her dogs in the Bois. Friends were uncertain, but for once impartial, and blamed both Jeannine and Andrée : 'One can't be sure that Andrée whistled for Jeannine, but those van-driver manners are very like her; that silly little Jeannine excels in organizing her slavery herself for the sadistic pleasure of snivelling from humiliation afterwards.'

After their quarrel they mourned in dignified and discreet fashion their close friendship which had lasted through two seasons at Deauville, two at Chamonix and three on the Riviera. Jeannine, the weaker, the cheekier and the more frivolous, went to a new dance-hall and invented a new little tea-place-bistro in Belleville where she took her friends at three o'clock in the afternoon, then at one o'clock in the morning, to eat potato salad and that strange fish, the sea-pike, which is sold in the flea-market and decried by aristocratic fishmongers because it has a jade-green backbone. Andrée, without Jeannine, returned to her country tastes, went for her walk in the Bois and her boating expedition on the lake one hour earlier. Jeannine thought, 'I'm drowning my sorrow', and Andrée, wearing her flat-heeled shoes, her Balaclava over her head and her hands in her pockets, repeated : 'Don't let anyone talk to me again about intimate friends, men or women ! I'm becoming once more the shy nymph of unexplored glades.'

Deep down within themselves they accepted, with naïve astonishment, their equal indifference, and the astonishing ease and harmlessness of their break.

The spring took Jeannine back to the restaurants in the Bois. May found her shivering in a cloak of white *crêpe*, dancing in order to keep warm, at eleven o'clock at night, on a floor white with electric moonlight, between the tables and the new trees creaking in the icy wind. She crossed the Bois whenever a day of errands authorized her to parade in faint, deceptive sunshine, wearing gauze in winter and furs in summer. But neither by night nor by day did the Bois remind her of her friend the nymph, for the morning Bois with its pedestrians is different from the evening Bois with its motor-cars.

It happened, however, that at the unusual hour of a quarter to twelve she was walking alone down one of the long pathways which lead from the Entre-Deux-Lacs to the waterfall. She was walking fast, for her new close woman friend, who was keen on sport, had just decided in favour of a game of tennis rather than her, and Jeannine, out of resentment, had refused the car. She was walking without pleasure, and did not hear the nightingales, nor the blackbirds and the orioles who try to imitate the nightingales. The acacias were losing their blossom, which snowed down in vain in Jeannine's path; her charming little nose, as imperious as the beak of a swift, was impervious to their scent, reminiscent of fritters tasting of vanilla and orange-flower water.

The sound of a whistle stopped her, and she knew why she stood still, as she heard through the undergrowth the cry 'Little dogs, little dogs, little dogs!' A Belgian sheepdog appeared, just long enough to show its bearlike eyes, its thick, low-hanging tail, like that of a she-wolf. A bulldog followed her, puffing like an old taxi, white in colour with a black monocle, shaped like a half-moon, then a frantic griffon terrier, bristling like a bundle of yellow straw.

'Mieke . . . Relaps . . . Joli-Blond . . .' counted Jeannine. After the dogs Andrée crossed the path, and did not see Jeannine, who recognized the chestnut-coloured waterproof suit, the muddy flat-heeled boots, the reddish-coloured woollen scarf and the whip with the thick plaited handle.

'Little dogs, little dogs, little dogs!'

The call faded; one of the dogs barked in the distance. Jeannine trembled as she stood motionless. She hoped for the familiar cry once more, heard nothing, and set off again slowly, with hesitation, her face pale and two tears remaining obstinately in her eyes.

'I wonder. . . . Really, I wonder what's the matter with me . . . I wonder. . . .' For nothing in her heart yearned for Andrée. She imagined quietly her 'slightly harem' scent, and her virile hands in the thick gloves. But deep down within her a jealous tenderness, a feeling of regret, smarting like the hurt felt by a child, demanded the three dogs who were so eager when out for a walk, the pleasure of calling them by their names, the right to put down two slender heels next to two low rubber heels on the damp pathway; the privilege of uttering, by the mist on the lake, by the full-blown, umbellate elder trees or the branch covered with tits, insignificant words whose only value lay in the time, the silly, pleasant tradition, the security of saying them again the next day.

Solitude made her weak again. She let herself moan quietly as she walked, stammering in a childish way.

'I want the dogs . . . I want the morning . . . I want to get up early . . . I want warm milk with rum, in the *buvette* near the lake, the day when it rained so hard . . . I want. . . .'

She turned round, waiting for a whim of Andrée's or the dogs to restore to the pathway the image of a time now out of reach, and found, without seeking it, the words formulating her wish and the expression of her distress: 'I want last year. . . .'

The Victim

For the first twelve months of the war it had been a daily struggle, for her and for us, to keep her alive, a kind of bitter game, or challenge to evil destiny. She was so pretty that all she need have done for a living, my goodness, was to sit back. But it was precisely this beauty, and then her situation as a young woman who had had her 'friend' killed in 1914, that filled us with compassion. We hoped to keep her fragile halo for her and during her widowhood give her first of all food and then that luxury : chastity.

This was a more difficult task than one might have thought, for we were dealing with the strangely fine feelings of an emotional suburban girl who was an honest business-woman. Josette agreed that everything can be bought and sold, even a disgusted breast, even an insensitive mouth. But a gift pure and simple made her suddenly angry and flushed with wounded pride : 'No, thank you ... I don't need it. ... No, we don't agree about the little bill for the jacket. I owed you fifty sous from last week. ...'

In order to prevent her from fading away or returning gloomily to a trade which disgusted her in advance we were obliged to make her sew, iron and cover lampshades. She only wanted to work in her own place, miles away, in a 'bedroom with boxroom', furnished mainly with photographs, where beneath a dismal, hygienic smell of coarse soap hung the distinctive perfume of a dark-haired girl with white skin.

During the winter of 1914 she would arrive gaily, bringing her work : 'It's me ! Don't let me disturb you !'

A toque, or some sort of hat, a narrow skirt which restricted her impatient steps, boots which had been turned inside-out and remade—for her little feet swam ironically in our shoes—and the rusty fur necklet that she preferred—it was more 'chic'!—to the coat that one of us had offered. And gloves!—but naturally! but always!—gloves. Her smooth beauty overcame this poverty. I've never encountered anything smoother than this child, whose black hair was never curled or waved, arranged artistically over smooth temples, and gleaming like valuable wood anointed with fine oil. Her pure, slightly prominent eyes, the supple cheeks, the mouth and chin seemed to tell everyone 'See how attractive we can be with the minimum of curliness.'

'I've brought back your little skirt,' explained Josette. 'I haven't edged the hem, it would have been stronger but it would have looked common. Just because there's a war on is no excuse for looking common, is it? And the blouse you wanted me to cut out of the evening coat, do you know what I found when I unpicked it? A hem turned in as much as that! Enough to make a big sailor collar to match!'

She shone with delight at being self-employed, at paying her way, at not being any liability. She had always 'had lunch before coming', and we used subterfuges to make her take away half a pound of chocolate.

'Josette, someone gave me this chocolate, I'm suspicious of it, it must be some drug. . . . Be a dear, try it, then tell me if it made you ill. . . .'

She accepted a sack of coal from Pierre Wolff, because I had told her that the playwright had noticed her when she was an extra at the Folies and still found the memory exciting.

She hardly ever spoke about her 'friend', an obscure actor

who had been killed by the enemy. But sometimes she looked at the pictures in the illustrated magazines of 1913 : 'Do you remember that revue? It was well staged, there isn't any. . . . And who'd believe my luck? The author was going to give me a small part in his next revue! It's a long way off, his next revue!'

One theatre half opened its doors, two theatres, ten theatres, and cinemas. Josette couldn't keep still.

'The Gobelins, the Montrouge and the Montparnasse are going to put on a season of plays, did you know? And then, the Moncey wants to put on a season of operetta, and the Levallois too. . . . The only thing, the thing that really matters, is to know whether the artists will be able to get the Métro home afterwards. At Levallois there won't be any Métro or tram, naturally. . . .'

She disappeared for three weeks and came back thinner, suffering from a cold, and proud of herself : 'I've got an engagement, Madame! *Miss Helyett* three times a week, I'll play one of the guides and possibly another small part too! Three times a week, and twice on Sundays!'

'How much will you get?'

She looked down.

'Oh, you know, *they're* taking advantage of the war . . . I get three francs fifty for each performance. The other days, naturally, we aren't paid. . . . And the show changes every fortnight, so we have to rehearse every day. . . . That's why I haven't had time to finish the little cami-knickers . . .'

'There's no hurry. . . . And how do you get home in the evenings?'

She laughed.

'Shanks's pony, naturally. An hour and a half's walk, I'll wear out more shoes than tyres. But they've told me that

I might possibly have a part in *Les Mousquetaires au couvent.* . . .'

How could we keep her back? She radiated freedom, zest, fatigue, and theatrical fever. . . . She went away, for months. . . .

*

In August 1916 I was buying a child's toy at one of those charity bazaars where they sell packets of coffee, necklaces of dyed wooden beads, raffia baskets and woollen things, and I was waiting for an elegant customer to leave me a space at the counter.

'That, that, yes, the blue jumper, and then the four bags of coffee,' she said. 'That will make us four separate parcels for the front, I'll write the addresses for you, Mademoiselle. I'll take the little baskets with me in my car . . .'

'In your car, Josette!'

'Oh, Madame, what a surprise! It's you I'm going to take in my car—yes, yes, I am, just for a moment, just the time to take you home. . . .'

She had not warned me that 'her' car already contained a well-turned-out man with barely greying hair, and she ordered him to unfasten one of the spare seats, for himself. She sat next to me and talked, trying to give the impression that she had forgotten the man's presence. He looked at her like a slave, but Josette's black eyes did not look at him even once. She removed one of her gloves and revealed scintillating rings; the man seized this fluttering hand and gave it a long kiss. She did not withdraw it but closed her eyes and only opened them again when he had raised his head. After a short silence the motor-car reached my house and Josette issued instructions to the man : 'Get out, then, you can see your seat's in the way, Madame can't get by.'

He obeyed at once, made his excuses and Josette, as she left me, promised she would come to see me : 'As soon as the rehearsals at the Edouard VII are over, I'll be there.'

She came a few days later, all in lawn and 'summer furs', a string of pearls round her neck and carrying a moiré handbag covered with brilliants. But she had not changed her coiffure in any way, and her unwaved, uncurled hair still lay flat over her temples as though she were a Japanese child.

'My little Josette, I don't need to ask what's happened to you. . . .'

She shook her head. 'Every misfortune, naturally! I've joined the ranks of the *nouveaux riches.*'

'So it seems. Are you in haricot beans or projectiles?'

'I'm in nothing—him . . . oh, he can buy or sell whatever he likes—the thing is, he doesn't interest me.'

'Now listen, for a military supplier he's very nice.'

'Yes, he's very nice. It's true all the same that he's very nice.'

She contemplated without seeing them her beautiful white suède shoes, and her face, although illuminated by pearls, snow-white lawn, pale fur and silk, seemed to have lost its glow.

'If I understand you correctly, Josette, you regret the time when . . .'

'Not at all,' she interrupted sharply. 'Don't imagine that! Why should I regret a time when I was cold, when I didn't have enough to eat, when I ran about in mud and snow, when without you and those other ladies I would have fallen ill or worse? Not at all! I belong to my country, I like what's good. Now that I no longer have anyone at the front except a few friends I look after in memory of Paul, why shouldn't I be the lady with the motor-car and the necklace, instead of the tenant downstairs? Fair's fair. By doing what I do I think I'm worth the blue fox furs and the tulle underwear. . . . That's certainly the least of it, since as far as that man's concerned, the man you saw, I'm the victim!'

I said nothing. Sensitively, she felt that these words were creating a gulf between us.

'Madame, Madame,' she exclaimed, 'you don't know. . . . You're blaming me . . . I swear to you, Madame . . .'

She nearly burst into tears and took a grip on herself.

'Madame, you've seen that man. You don't have to have second sight to understand that there's no better man than he is. Madame, he's good. Madame, he's sensitive, and well groomed, he's everything—which doesn't stop me from being the victim.'

'But why, my child?'

'Why? But quite simply because I don't love him, and I'll never love him, Madame. If he were ugly and revolting and stingy, I'd console myself, I'd tell myself : "It's quite natural that I can't bear the sight of him. He's bought me, I hate him, it's quite normal." But Madame, that man, I don't love him because I don't love him, oh my goodness, how unhappy I'm making myself because of him. . . .'

She was silent a moment, searching for words, examples.

'Now look, the day before yesterday he gave me this ring. And so nicely! Then, I began to cry. . . . He called me "My sensitive little girl!" and I cried thinking of the pleasure I'd have felt on receiving a ring from someone I loved, and I was angry with him, I was so angry with him I could have bitten him. . . .!'

'What a child you are, Josette. . . .'

She struck the arm of the chair in irritation.

'No, Madame, you're wrong, forgive me! One is not such a child as that, in Paris, at twenty-five. I know what love is, I've been through it. I have a very loving nature, although it doesn't show. The result is I consider myself the victim of that man, and I'm jealous of him, so jealous it makes me ill.'

'Jealous?'

'Yes, envious. I envy everything he has, and which I can't have, for he's in love. The other day the little Peloux girl said to me at rehearsal, "Your friend has a nice mouth, he must kiss well." "I've no idea," I replied. And it's true that I've no idea, I shan't know. The woman who finds him attractive will know. I shall die without knowing whether he kisses well or badly, if he makes love well or badly. When he kisses me my mouth becomes like . . . like nothing. It's dead, it feels nothing. My body too. But as for him, the little I give him—you should see his face, his eyes. Ah, he gets a thousand times more from it than I do! Ten thousand times more!

'Then you can imagine, one's nerves. . . . Sometimes I'm unkind, I take my revenge, I'm sharp with him. Once I was so unkind that he wept. That was the last straw! If I'd said another word I'd have gone too far. The trouble is that I know what it's like to have someone in your life who's only to say one word to make you feel in heaven or hell. I'm that someone for him. He has everything, Madame, he has everything! And he can't do a single thing for me, Madame, not a thing—he can't even make me unhappy!'

She began to sob and her words came through her violent tears. 'Tell me, Madame, am I wrong, tell me?' But I couldn't find anything—and I haven't found anything since —to say to her.

My Friend Valentine

My dear Valentine,

I received your postcard. I succeeded in making out—in the few lines which cover the view of the Lac du Bourget like a network of fine hairs—the faithful friendliness and affectionate concern it expresses.

We parted somewhat coolly, and you write to me in circumspect fashion : 'Weather terrible, outings impossible, we're thinking of coming home. . . . And what are you doing?'

That's enough : I translate without difficulty : 'I'm afraid I've upset you completely. . . . Don't forget me, don't be cross with me; we haven't two ideas in common, but I'm fond of you, I don't know why; I like you just as you are, with all your faults. I'm anxious about you : reassure me. . . .'

Don't blush, dear Valentine—it makes one's face-powder come off !—and understand at once that I'm still your friend.

I've followed your movements from the newspapers. The *Figaro* told me of your presence in Trouville, and some fashionable feminist paper described you in surprising terms: you were said to be wearing 'a navy blue Louis XV suit, faultless, with guayaquil looped with rose pink. . . .' Guayaquil looped with rose pink ! Really ! As a friend of mine used to say, a certain Claudine, 'I don't know what it is, but it must be beautiful !'

Because I'm living in a desert of yellow sand—square miles of sea-shore, without a blade of green, without a single pebble, I'm surprised, in my simple way, that there are still ladies who wear hats, tight-fitting dresses, boned collars, long corsets and dangerous slender heels. . . . How can I admit to you that I've put away my skirts and shoes for the season, and that I walk with insensitive, horny bare feet over the varnished seaweed, the knife-edged shells and the grey, salty whin that breaks through the sand? How dare I describe myself to you, with my blackened skin, my nose slightly peeling from too much sun, my arms covered with fast-dye dark brown? Thank goodness the sea-mews and the gulls and the delightful curlews are the only ones to be frightened by my riding kit : knickerbockers which used to be blue, and a coarse knitted jersey. Add to this cyclist's stockings, rubber shoes, a cap that has gone soft, and the whole thing seated astride a big bay horse—and you will have a little equestrian group that would never be seen at the corner of the Bois.

At least let me congratulate you ! *Femina* reproduces your portrait, in a tennis dress, among those of the 'best tennis players' at Deauville. . . . It's delightful, this Joan of Arc cuirass in white serge, cutting across the pleated skirt half-way up the thighs. In that costume you have a slightly warlike look, nothing whatever to do with sport, but so attractive !

You see, we're no longer cross with each other at all, we two. You're so unbearable, my dear Valentine, and I'm so impossible ! I can still see us, exchanging in highly dignified fashion a courteous and theatrical farewell. You had asked me 'what I was doing this summer' and I'd answered : 'But . . . first of all I'm going to act in *La Chair*[1] at Marseille.' To which you replied : 'Again !'

---

[1] *La Chair* (Flesh), a mime drama in which the young Colette, partnered by the famous mime Georges Wague, scored her first success on the stage.

I : What do you mean, 'again'?

You : That ghastly thing again!

I : It's not ghastly, it's a 'sensational mime drama'.

You : It's ghastly, really! It's in that piece, isn't it, that they tear your dress off and you appear . . .

I : Without a dress, precisely.

You : And doesn't that mean anything to you?

I : In what way?

You : Exposing yourself in public in a get-up, in a costume . . . well. . . . It's beyond me! When I think that you stand there in front of everyone . . . oh!

You were overcome with an irresistible shudder of modesty, you put both hands over your face, your whole body recoiled so far that your dress clung to you and for a moment revealed you more than naked : your little breasts crushed by a tight-fitting corset, your stomach elongated and flat, ending in a mysterious fold, your thighs rounded and close together, your knees delicate, slightly bent, every detail of your graceful body appeared to me so clearly beneath the *crêpe de Chine* that I was embarrassed. . . .

But you were already uncovering your angry eyes : 'I've never seen . . . unconcern like yours, Colette !'

To which I replied with coarseness devoid of wit : 'My child, you bore me. You're neither my mother nor my lover: therefore . . .'

An angry sigh, a stiff handshake, and that was our goodbye. Now I laugh to myself as I think of your special modesty which shelters beneath vast, deep-crowned hats a slender body whose every step reveals beneath a tight, short tunic the movement of the hips, the roll of the tight, protruding buttocks and even the pink and amber colour of the arms. I very much want to take you to task a little, you who—not content to appear in broad daylight in this costume that a little Tanagra nymph would have found barely adequate, you who emerge from the sea at Trouville, your nipples visible beneath the taut silk bathing-dress which gleams like a wet fish . . .

There's one thing, my dear Valentine, that you'll never teach me : it's that the skin right down on my back or my hips can be more tempting and secret than the skin on my hand or my calf, and it's this 'unconcern', as you call it, this primitive serenity which makes all your indignation, all your display of trifling virtue—local virtue, if I may say so—your modesty measured in square inches, seem pointless.

Do you remember the famous police proceedings against nudity in the music-hall? One little walker-on was cruelly upset at this period. She was playing two parts in a December review : one showed her nude, chaste and silent, motionless on a cardboard cloud, with a bow in her hand. Two tableaux later she came back on stage with 'feminine underwear', dressed in a lace petticoat and a pair of socks : her little naked knees would tremble as she sang a song with indistinct words, and the flowers of her breasts showed mauve through the lawn. She was sweet in those clothes, slightly ridiculous, and totally indecent; as a result, one of her two roles was cut : understand by that that she relinquished the bow of Artemis and kept her petticoat !

Does that seem quite natural to you?

I was sure of it.

O you wretched little creature ! There are, however, moments when I am weak enough to want you to understand me, when I want to seize hold of your golden hair—real and false on that little head that's harder than a coco-nut, and to knock it very hard, to shake out of it all the prejudices, all the remnants of ideas, the débris of principles that together make such an immoral racket inside it . . .

Yes, immoral, little blockhead! Immoral, you silly! Immoral, you mindless creature! (And I'm even using proper words! . . .) I don't mind your round eyes and your horrified mouth. You'll never know how ill I think of you, you who look at me because I've stopped having a husband, as though I'd contracted an embarrassing disease, hard to conceal and hard to admit. You'll laugh, as though it were some easy paradox, if I try to explain to you that the state of marriage appears to me preposterous and rather abnormal, you who have a husband—a husband in motor-cars!—and who forget, while on his arm, unfaithfulness, the flight of a first lover. . . .

Haven't you ever contemplated that man, your husband, deeply, and at length? Don't reply, in witty, evasive fashion, 'Yes, since I've been unfaithful to him!' Remember, without laughing, the time when you were never unfaithful to him. Was there not a day in your life when you were faithful and loving, even in love, when you looked at him suddenly, with a feeling of astonishment: 'What's this man doing in my house, with me? Why in fact do I live with *this Man* who's there, in my bedroom? I married him, fine! I've been to bed with him, fine!—all of which doesn't alter the fact that he's *a Man*, a Man like any other, who's there in my room, in my bed, in my life. . . . He comes in to see me, into my *cabinet de toilette*, after asking "I'm not disturbing you, darling?" I reply "No, my love!" but that doesn't alter the fact that *this Man* is there, in my room, and that doesn't alter the fact that his face, the shape of his back, the way he strokes his moustache, suddenly appear to me all at once as strange, shocking, out of place. . . . All my life, then, I shall live like this *with a Man*, who will have the right to see how awful I look in the morning, to come in while I'm drinking my laxative *tisane*, will ask about the awkward dates in my little feminine calendar, will walk about in his underpants in my *cabinet de toilette*! . . . He's there in my life, for the whole of life! Why? I don't know, in fact! I love him . . . but that's another matter : love has nothing to do with living together—on the contrary, it usually dies as a result.'

Admit it, my dear Valentine, it's not possible that your state of marriage hasn't revealed itself to you—for an hour, for a moment—in all its preposterous vulgarity! And who can say that your husband too hasn't suffered from it in his own modest way, man's modesty is nearly always more sensitive and sincere than ours? I mean your husband, mine, everyone's husband. . . . One morning he wakes up in a gloomy mood, absent-minded, hardly saying a word, his eyes downcast. . . . When, kindly, you ask him 'What's the matter, darling?' he replies 'Nothing . . . a touch of migraine . . .' and after swallowing the *pyramidon* that you affectionately offer him, he remains silent, with the expression of a man to whom something has happened.

What has happened to him is the same thing that has happened to you! He doesn't know you. He looks at you surreptitiously over his newspaper, astonished and disgusted, in fact, at suddenly discovering you, on taking apart, with a cold lucid glance, this woman who is there in his house, who sings to herself as she pushes tortoise-shell hairpins into her chignon, rings for the maid, gives orders, makes decisions, arranges things. . . . I assure you, my friend, that during these fleeting moments there are looks from lover to mistress, from wife to husband, that are frightening. . . .

I remember a delightful remark by my mother, who was

being admonished one day by my father in pretty strong terms.

'I forbid you,' she told him, 'to speak to me like that: you're not even related to me!'

My childish ears remembered this unusual remark, and since then I often thought about it. . . .

You're quite capable at this moment, you little pest, of reading this with a nice, wicked smile which means: 'It's understandable she hasn't a good word to say for marriage, she who . . .' I who what? I who can't congratulate myself about it? That's a fine thing! I insist on not letting you sidestep the question in a feminine way. I will quote you something that has remained very much in my mind, the little sermon that my mother read me the day before I married the man I loved, and who loved me.[2]

'So, my poor little pet, you're going to leave me? You're going to go away, and who with?'

'But Mama, with the man I love!'

'I know very well you love him, and that's not the best part of your story. In fact it would be better if you loved him less. And what happens afterwards?'

'Afterwards? Nothing.'

'Nothing. You're far gone. The thing I see most clearly is that you're going to go away with a man, and I don't find that very wonderful, my daughter going away with a man.'

'But Mama, he'll be my husband!'

[2] Colette herself could well have had this discussion with her mother before she left home at the age of twenty (in 1893) to marry Henri Gauthier-Villars, critic and writer of light novels, which he signed 'Willy'.

'That means nothing to me, the fact that he'll be your husband. I've had two husbands, and I'm no better off as a result. . . . A man whom you don't even know!'

'Oh, but I do, Mama, I do know him!'

'You don't know him, you little silly, because you love him! You're going to go away, all alone, with a man, and your brothers and I will watch you go, with very long faces. It's disgusting that such things should be allowed!'

'But really, Mama, you're extraordinary. What do you want me to do?'

'What you want to do, naturally. But it's not nice. Everything's so badly arranged. Now look! He tells you he loves you and, since you love him too, there you are in his arms and ready to follow him to the ends of the earth. But let him say to you suddenly "I don't love you", he looks different to you! You discover that he has the short nose of people who lack judgment and balance, and the short, thick neck of those who commit murder when they're angry, the modulated and seductive voice of a liar, the chin of a weak and sensual woman. . . . My darling little pet, don't cry! I'm only an old kill-joy. What can I do? I always say outrageous things, but the truth is that you'd have to marry your own brother if you wanted to know what you're doing, and even then. . . . All this strange blood that comes into a family, it means that you look at your own son and say "Where does he get those eyes, and that forehead, and those wild fits of anger, and that skill in lying?" Ah, my poor darling pet, I'm not trying to explain, or to create a new society, as they say, but everything's so badly arranged!'

My dear Valentine, forgive me, I'm letting myself be carried away by memories that are hardly gay. I'm not trying to change anything that exists, any more than my delightful crazy mother was doing. Solitude, intoxicating freedom and the absence of any corset have made me, as you see, a preacher of the worst type. I only wanted to moralize a little, in my turn, out of a pure desire to tease.

And I enter the game with a lamentable conviction. I seem to see, within ten years or so, an old, dried-up, argumentative Colette with hair like a Russian girl student, wearing reformist dress, who will go into the towns urging free love, proud isolation and so on and so forth, and a lot of nonsense! Brr . . .! But what demon shows me something even more terrible, the image of an eighty-year-old Colette, burning with a new love, mature and yielding beneath her make-up, militant and desperate? With both arms outstretched I repulse the two apparitions, I search between the two of them for a sheltered narrow path, where a friendly hand will guide me. . . .

Goodbye, my dear. I'm afraid really you won't like this letter. We'll never agree, dear Valentine. And all our lives, I hope, we'll look for each other, with an aggressive, disinterested tenderness. You no longer hope you will bring me back to 'the right road', I don't count on converting you. That gives our conversations an artificial and inoffensive warmth, which brings comfort and no illusions.

Goodbye! go back to your tennis, in the Joan of Arc cuirass dress. I'm off to fish for flatfish which you find beneath your bare feet, in the deep holes left by the low tide. There's a high wind, the sand blows along in long swift streams which run parallel to the horizon, and their crawling movement makes me dizzy. Beneath the low sky the shore is an endless desert, the colour of ash, and the pale dunes smoke beneath the wind which destroys them. . . . You would die of misery here, my child, and yet I like it . . . I kiss you; come back beautiful and happy.

Your friend
Colette Willy

*

What has to happen, happens. . . . Accused of every sin, I appeared before my friend Valentine, after receiving an enigmatic telegram: I'VE MUCH TO SCOLD YOU ABOUT. YOU'RE BREAKING MY HEART.

How could an unworthy creature like me cause heartbreak to this tall young woman who was so well dressed, no doubt sewn into her woollen dress so that she could neither sit down, bend, nor walk properly . . . oh, for the gold chain which regulated Salammbô's walk. . . .

I've broken my friend Valentine's heart. . . . What have I done now? My pretty judge in her black dress and lace jabot shows the embarrassment felt by all judges, and I wouldn't be in her place.

'Come on, Valentine. Aren't you going to take your cap off?'

For she's wearing a cap, a sort of bathing-cap for elegant bathing, made out of some twisted gleaming stuff. Her ears are invisible; so is her hair, apart from one blonde lock over the right temple. It's neat, slightly reminiscent of Saint-Lazare, very attractive. I indicated the object with circumspection: 'What's it made of, precisely?'

'Wood,' replied my friend Valentine, anxious to delay my appearance in court. 'Woven wood, which is then plunged into a bath of adhesive silver.'

'Adhesive, my dear girl!'

'Adhesive. And the stuff draped round it is pale blue American cloth.'*

'It's been launched for the Monte Carlo season, along with the large dinner hat in light leather. It's very new. I can't say it's terribly attractive. . . .'

'No, you can't. But tell me why you've come, what's behind this alarming telegram.'

The young woman in the cap gathered herself together, drew a remarkable degree of courage from the depths of her being and said : 'Well, it's this. The day before yesterday you had dinner at the Sémiramis Bar.'

'That's true. So what?'

'So what? That's all. Isn't that enough?'

'Yes, that's enough, for I have dinner there two or three times a week. The food's good.'

The aigrette—what could it be made of? steel wool?—which surmounted the cap of woven wood and American cloth, quivered, danced and bowed.

'But, you wretched woman, it's a place . . . a place . . .'

'With a bad reputation. Indeed it is.'

My poor friend Valentine abandoned declamatory methods. She looked at me with a sudden gentleness, superior in her solicitude.

'One could really say, you poor dear, that you want to make it impossible for your friends to stick up for you . . .'

'Who asked you to do that? I certainly didn't.'

'I mean, well . . . you know I'm very fond of you. What do you expect me to say when someone tells me you've been having dinner at the Sémiramis Bar?'

'Tell them the truth—it's none of your business.'

---

* I'm not making it up.

My poor little judge blushed and hesitated. It's much easier to be the accused. I enjoy it, I settle into it, I subside into the most voluptuous of my faults and Valentine lacks the confidence to prise me away from them.

'Obviously it's none of my business. It's in your interest. . . . This sort of thing could do you harm. You seem to be trying on purpose to. . . . And then, if you just went there *en passant*, all right. . . . But it's quite a different thing to become an habituée, a sort of club member. If at least you went there with a party, sometimes. . . . But you sit in a corner all alone, with your newspaper and your dog, and all those people say good day to you, those young men with long jackets, rings, and bracelets round their ankles. . . . And then,' she added, growing bolder, 'I've been told that the suppers there are . . . terrible!'

'I don't know anything about them, my dear. I don't have supper.'

'That's true, you don't have supper. But you know, don't you, that the suppers . . .'

'Yes, I know. Sémiramis tells me about them.'

'She tells you . . .'

'Of course. Sémiramis is a fine type. Don't you know her? Haven't you ever seen her little snub nose, it makes her look like a bulldog, and she has a chestnut-coloured chignon, a fringe like the peak on a cap and a bosom like a Spanish balcony.'

'I haven't had the pleasure . . .'

'Too bad. She's insolent, kind-hearted, patient and idiotically healthy. She doesn't charge much for the leek soup, the chicken with sausages and the loin of veal—she even gives it all away to a whole mob of hard-up types in long jackets, and poor girls all dolled up. At her place they can get food

and the *thune*. . . . The *thune*, Valentine, is a five-franc
piece . . .'

'Oh, I know that. Everyone knows that, obviously . . .'

'Sorry. So you see, Sémiramis wears a helmet, and her
armour consists of an apron with pockets. Like this she reigns
over her so-called ill-famed bar. And the way you and everyone else see it, ill-famed it is.'

'I certainly hope so.'

'So do I. She knows the names of all her regulars, and the
names of all the girls' boy friends. She's no love for people
she doesn't know and when casual customers come in she
barks at them, "You can't feed your faces here!" She knows
the gossip and scandal from all the other bars and she's discreet about it. One day Sémiramis told me the sad and
scandalous story of a little woman sitting there—without my
asking her—and afterwards she added : "I'm the only person
who knows her story, she'd be horribly upset if anyone else
in Paris knew it!"'

'Delightful.'

'You don't find that sort of thing every day! At least in
the case of Sémiramis it's only thoughtlessness. And then,
what can I do, my dear, I'm a home bird, I'm a bit fussy and
I like to be quiet. I often have to eat out, before going to the
theatre, I don't enjoy going to a restaurant on the boulevards,
nor into a fashionable grill-room where everyone whispers
about each other, pulls them to bits and runs them down.
I go to Sémiramis, who's well named, Sémiramis the warrior
queen, with her bronze helmet and her carving knife; she
talks to her clientele in colourful language—young men with
long hair and women with short hair . . .'

'That's just the clientele I'm scolding you about!'

'Why?'

'Every night, in that bar, there are scenes, orgies, even fights . . .'

'I'll say it again, I don't know anything about that. What does it matter to me? The orgies in the Sémiramis Bar must be like all orgies, boring enough to make the most hysterical people virtuous. I'm only interested in the people who have dinner there. They're the ones I want to talk to you about, Valentine, since I'm kindly consenting to give an explanation. . . . Yes, you'll find a large number of young men who aren't the slightest bit interested in women. At dinner-time they feel at home there, they're resting. They're gathering strength for supper. They don't need to waggle their hips, call out shrilly, wave handkerchiefs moistened with ether, or dance together, or to shout loudly "Sémiramis, another sherry for me, on Monsieur's bill!" They're relaxed and weary, and their made-up eyes reveal their lack of sleep. One man who's taken the name of an authentic princess demands Vittel water, and lots of leeks in his soup because they cleanse the blood. Another one, with the face of an anaemic little girl, gets his broth and noodles at Sémiramis's place, and the harsh sovereign fills his plate twice, like a grumpy mother. One lanky boy with hallucinated blue eyes pushes his plate away untouched; Sémiramis puts her hands on her hips and exclaims, "You've been fixing yourself with morphine again, have you? What's your mother doing, letting you kill yourself like this? Hasn't she got a heart?" There's another who looks like Suzanne Derval, with his violet eyes and innocent nose; he picks at his food and says, "For heaven's sake, no sauce. I don't want to ruin my stomach! Waiter, once and for all, take away those pickles and let me have my benzonaphtol tablets!"

'There they are, they're nice, they're unaffected, they're

idle and fed up, like prostitutes out of work, but they laugh
easily and play with the dog Sémiramis found in the street
one night. . . . If some strange person sneaks in for dinner
they become uneasy, they behave in the grumpy manner of
shopkeepers who've been roused too early. From one table to
another they exchange sounds like cocks crowing, forced
laughter, obscene platitudes, patter, in fact, that attracts
attention. . . . The customer, or the group of drinkers and
inquisitive ones swallow their beer or sip kümmel on ice, then
the door closes behind them. There's a whoop of relief, followed by calm and quiet chat, and the young men with their
narrow chests decked out with loud ties and gaudy pocket
handkerchiefs lean against the tables again, in lazy relaxa-
tion, like circus animals after exercise. . . .'

Valentine doesn't much like it if people talk to her for any
length of time. After a few moments of concentration the
animation and brightness fade from her face and give way
to a rigid look, a sleepy attempt to keep her eyes open. . . .
I stopped talking. But she certainly hadn't finished.

'That's all very fine. When you want to plead not guilty
you dress it all up with literature and you say to yourself :
"If I talk rather fast and put some nice words in it Valentine
will be taken in." It's easier than sending me away, isn't it?'

This kindness and feminine cunning always disarm me,
and my friend Valentine, who often infuriates me, sometimes
surprises me, as though I had suddenly noticed beneath her
coiffure with its coils of artificial hair, beneath her hats
reminiscent of saucepans or the *grandes eaux* at Versailles,
the pointed tip of an ear like some crafty little animal . . . I
can't help laughing.

'But I'm not defending myself, you little horror! What or
whom would I be defending myself against? Against you?

Would I condescend to do that, you little megalomaniac!'

She pouted in her seductive way, as though some man were making advances to her.

'You see! You see! I'm the one who's going to be in trouble! It's too much! Because I took the liberty of saying that the Sémiramis Bar wasn't exactly a branch of a convent and because I spoke disrespectfully of that Queen of Babylon and other places!'

'Sémiramis doesn't ask for respect. What would she do with it? It can't be eaten, it can't be sold and it takes up space. But she dispenses to me a scrap of that grumpy maternal feeling which turns her habitués into a crowd of spoilt children, who are hustled about and well behaved. . . . In any case, her uncertain temper, which is both fierce and generous at the same time, makes her in my view worthy of an authentic sceptre. "What do I owe you, Sémiramis?" I once heard a wretched, anxious-looking girl habituée ask her in a low voice. "I don't know. I haven't done your account," Sémiramis grumbled. "Do you think you're the only one I've got to deal with?" "But I've got money this evening, Sémiramis . . ." "Money, money . . . you're not the only one who's got money!" "But Sémiramis . . ." "Oh, stop bothering me, I'll always manage, you know. The customer at the back table has just paid me a louis for his chicken casserole, a hundred sous more than at Paillard's place, look at his ugly face, he's just leaving. Monsieur didn't want anything on my menu! Monsieur orders different things for himself! Monsieur believes he's in a restaurant!" As she said this her fierce brown eyes glared at the terrified back of the escaping diner who thought that a louis gave him the right to eat chicken casserole at Sémiramis's place. . . . Am I boring you, Valentine?'

'Not at all, anything but.'

'That's more than I hoped for! I'm a success. I've the
courage to tell you now that I find pleasure, while I'm
having dinner at Sémiramis's place, in looking at women in
each other's arms, waltzing well. They're not paid for that,
and they dance for their own pleasure, between the cabbage
soup and the *boeuf bourguignonne*. They're young models,
little good-time girls living locally, little music-hall artists
out of work. . . . I can't see the dancers' faces under their big
cartwheel hats or the cloche caps pulled down to their eyes,
I can forget the odd little faces, the slightly protruding jaws,
blue with powder. I can only see two graceful bodies linked
together, their shapes moulded beneath their thin dresses by
the wind stirred up by the waltzing, two thin, lanky adolescent bodies with delicate feet clad in thin shoes, and they've
come through the snow and mud without a car. . . . They
waltz like girls who go regularly to dances in the street, with
coarse, languorous movements, leaning over delectably like
a high sail on a yacht . . . I find it more attractive than a
ballet. . . . That's the moment, my dear Valentine, when I
leave the Sémiramis Bar, but Sémiramis herself sometimes
makes a conspiratorial sign to me and stops me at the door—
"Hush, don't say a word," she whispered the other evening,
putting the string of a bulging parcel round my finger.
"Don't say a word, it's some apples I've dug out for you,
the old russets you like, they're as wrinkled as a beggar's
bottom. . . ." I suppose that makes you laugh? I thought it
very nice. She knew that I like the old, crinkled, musky
apples, smelling like the storeroom where I used to arrange
them when I was a child . . .'

'Of course it's nice,' my friend agreed. 'And now I'm off.
But you know, I'm not discouraged! I'll be back again to

moralize to you. I'll seek you out again, I will ! . . . I'll seek you out, you bad lot!'

'At the *Sémiramis Bar*, this evening, at eight o'clock.'

'At the Sémiramis Bar, this evening at eight o'clock, if you like.'

With her hand on the doorknob, she turned round. Her eyes were laughing beneath the blonde lock, and this was all I could see of her between her cap which was pulled down low at the back of her head and a sort of ermine scarf wound twice round her neck.

'Tell me, in fact, do you think my husband would know, if I went to have dinner there at the same time as you, wearing a dark dress and a respectable hat?'

*

'Now if I had a daughter . . .'

'But you haven't a daughter!'

My friend Valentine shrugged her shoulders in irritation. I'd broken one of the rules of her favourite game : the game of *if I had*. I already knew how this peremptory young woman would behave *if* she had a motor-car, *if* she had a yacht, *if* her husband were Minister of War, *if* she inherited ten millions, *if* she were a great actress. . . .

When she comes to my house I feel the wind rising and I half close my eyes as though I were by the sea. She comes in breathless and looks round.

'You can say what you like,' she murmurs each time, 'your place in Passy is at the end of the world!'

Even if she invited me there, I wouldn't say what I liked . . . but I allow her to tell me everything that goes through her head.

Ever since the appearance of the Russian ballet my friend
Valentine has worn, in a stiff manner, fashionable clothes
which might be just tolerable on someone with the smoothest
Oriental grace. She uses rose and jasmin scents, swears by
Teheran and Ispahan, and she doesn't hesitate—while wearing a Byzantine dress brightened by a Marie-Antoinette
fichu, a Cossack cap and American shoes shaped like sabots
—to exclaim : 'How can one not be Persian?'

She knows her own mind, is fickle and fierce. As soon as
she crosses the threshold she hurls floods of words at me,
endless strings of contradictory axioms. She values me because I don't struggle, and she readily thinks I'm shy when
I'm only exhausted. She talks while I read and while I
write. . . . Today, the mild and rainy autumn afternoon
brings her to me quite subdued and formal . . . she's acting
the bourgeoise who rears in despotic fashion the children she
hasn't got.

'If I had a daughter—then, my dear, I'd show people
what I think of the modern ways of bringing up the young,
and the mania for sport, and girls in the American style!
They make rotten wives, you know, and hopeless mothers!
What are you looking at in the garden?'

'Nothing.'

Nothing. . . . I'm silently asking the russet trees and the
softened earth, where my friend Valentine has got her infor-
mation about modern methods of bringing up the young—
I'm not looking at anything except my neighbours' narrow
garden and their house, a brick and wooden chalet forgotten
in Passy among the farthest gardens. . . .

'A return to family life, my dear, it's the only thing! And
family life as our grandmothers understood it! They didn't

worry about *baccalauréats* for girls in those days and nobody was any the worse for it, anything but!'

I looked up for a moment at my houri in her green caftan, searching in vain for any trace of a lurking *baccalauréat* from which she'd never quite recovered.

'Yes, I assure you that if I had a daughter I'd make her into a little provincial girl, healthy and quiet in the old style. A little piano-playing, not too much reading, but lots of sewing! She'd know how to mend, embroider, look after linen. My dear, I can see her as though she were there, my daughter! Her hair brushed smooth, with a flat collar . . . I assure you, I can see her!'

I can see her too. She has just sat down, as she does every afternoon, in the house next door, by the window: she's almost a child, with smooth-brushed hair and a pale complexion, her eyes lowered over some embroidery . . .

'I'd dress her in those little fabrics, you know, which have a rather dark background and silly little patterns on them. She'd certainly have a terrific success in them! And every day, every day, instead of courses at the Sorbonne or fashionable lectures, she'd sit near a window, or by a lamp—I've got a little oil lamp, actually, in decorated porcelain, it's sweet! —she would sit down with her embroidery or her crochet. A young girl who plies her needle doesn't want to go astray, you know!'

What does that girl think about it? I can see nothing of her at the moment except her dark smooth hair fastened at the back of her neck with a black ribbon. Her hand moves backwards and forwards with concentration, working with a long thread, and it flutters like a bird at the end of a string . . .

My friend Valentine utters a peroration, at the height of her attack of platonic motherhood: 'Ladies' needlework, yes, my dear, ladies' needlework! People have laughed at it long enough, without realizing that in the past this was the cause of much family stability, and the moral well-being of many adolescents!'

The child who's embroidering in the little house has raised her head. She looks at the damp garden where wet leaves are raining down, but does not seem to see it. She has deep and serious eyes, dark eyeballs which are the only moving thing in her motionless face . . .

'Don't you agree with me, actually?'

. . . velvety, large eyeballs whose gaze wanders over the garden, seeking a patch of sky between the trees, and turn distrustfully to the room that is drowned in shadow . . .

'Oh, when it's one of your absent-minded days nobody can pin you down. Goodbye, I'm cross. Yes, I'm very cross.'

. . . and return to the embroidery she had begun, sheltered beneath their long eyelids. . . . Every day this dark-haired child sits and embroiders until it is time to light the lamps.

If the weather's fine, her window is open, and as dusk falls I hear a voice calling her: 'Lucie! Come on now, you'll harm your eyes!'

Regretfully she leaves her chair and her light work—and I wait until the next day for the reappearance, against the vague background of an old-fashioned room, of this pretty phantom from my distant adolescence . . .

A provincial girl with smooth-brushed hair, plying her needle. . . . She's very good, isn't she? And voluntarily silent, and not very inquisitive . . . does one call her a 'waking dreamer'? Does she go to her low chair as to the entrance of the forbidden garden which she enters alone, each day, before the blind eyes of those who surround her? Between them and the dangerous countries where she wanders does she unfold, as though to prevent access by everyone, the handkerchief she's scalloping, or the stiff canvas? . . .

Ladies' needlework, the safety of confident mothers. . . . What bad book can equal, for a solitary girl, the long silence, the limitless dreaming over the openwork muslin or by the rosewood loom? Bad books may be frightening, if they are too realistic, or else they disappoint. . . . But dreaming leaps forward boldly, cunning, impudent and varied, to the rhythm of the needle which bites into the silk; dreaming grows, its burning wing beats in the silence, enflames the pale little hand, and the cheek where the shadows of the eyelashes quiver. Dreaming fades away, retreats, seems to dissolve when a word is spoken aloud, when a thread breaks, when a ball of silk rolls on to the floor—the dream becomes diaphanous and from time to time allows the family background, the passer-by outside the window to show through; but the new needleful, the virgin canvas, the work taken up again ensure its return, and it is the dream, always the dream, that causes so many little girls to bend their heads in concentration, it is the dream which secretly dwells within so many 'waking dreamers', it is this I recognize in my neighbour's gaze, the girl with her head bent, this beautiful feminine gaze, absent-mindedly moving within a motionless face. . . .

*

'You don't mind if I dress while you're here?'

'Not at all.'

'That's nice of you . . . I'm so pleased to see you,' added my friend Valentine.

But I can see her reflection in the slanting mirror, her

reflection with which she has just exchanged an anxious look, an irritable movement of her eyebrows . . . I'm annoying her . . . I've come at a bad moment. . . . She's wishing me in hell. . . . Even farther away : in the depths of Passy, where I live ! She wishes me there, she's installing me there and locking me in, with a book on my knee, in front of a good summer fire . . .

'You see,' she finished aloud, somewhat ingeniously, 'I'm going out to dinner and we're all going together to the dress rehearsal of *La Grande Glycine*, so . . .'

'Don't talk, get dressed as though I weren't here.'

In fact she threw off her dress and her little knickers, her Valenciennes lace brassière, scratched her bare arms, stroked her rumpled chemise with the flat of her hand, with the shocking immodesty of one woman undressing in front of another. But she retreated into darkness and mystery to take off her shoes, in a corner, with her back turned. She regained confidence with a pair of purple tulle stockings and two shoes glittering with gold, so beautiful that my friend smiled at them affectionately as she walked round the bedroom, gracefully and lightly clad, hesitating on her high heels. A darting pain pulled down the corners of her mouth and she uttered a common expression quite sincerely, 'Ouch, my feet . . .' as she collapsed in front of the dressing table. . . .

The task which was to follow was familiar to me : it was the skilful, almost theatrical make-up which completes young women-about-town who care about fashion, and makes them look conventional. I say young women, for the others use more discretion over it, leaving to their younger sisters the feverish taste for crude make-up, the delight of children messing about with colours, fingering the white, red and blue and covering themselves with it up to the ears.

I took great care not to open my mouth. There would be time for everything, and I knew that one doesn't gossip while doing one's face. I had to be content with the sounds indicating impatience and the fragments of sentences which my friend Valentine uttered, like little scraps of cotton wool which she passed over her cheeks and eyelids and then threw away. . . .

'Is everything all right with you? . . . Good. . . . It's odd all the same that I can't get my maid to fill up my pot of cold cream when it's empty. . . . I beg you, my dear, tell me that it isn't eight o'clock yet or I'll go mad! . . . So everything's all right with you? . . . Naturally, when I want to be quick I spoil the tip of my nose. . . . No, I haven't got too much rouge on. . . . I beg you, my dear, don't talk to me just now, I'll get mascara in my eye. . . .'

Theatre work and chatter, the nervousness of an actress afraid of missing her entrance. . . . Were it not for the elegance of the boudoir, one could be taken in. I made just sufficient reply for my friend to be almost oblivious of my presence, so that I could follow and take in the transformations in her slanting reflection. . . .

To start with, here's her real face, completely naked, cleansed with vaseline, the face her mother gave her. She shows it to her husband, her maid, and to me, for I'm not important either. It's a little blonde face, lit up by blue eyes; the eyelids are tired and there's slight congestion at the cheekbones and the nostrils. The eyelashes are very fair and must gleam in the sun like crushed glass—but when do they see the sun? They're about to receive once more their artificial blackness and stiffening. My friend had just firmly embedded a comb in her delicately coloured, almost pink hair, to hold it back. Within the silver frame of the mirror the total effect is luminous, charmingly clear-cut, pale and distinguished. That slender neck needs a white collar of fairly stiff lace, cool to the eye. The comb, which was stuck in sideways for this rapid *toilette*, should sink more deeply into the beautiful hair, holding it tightly together, polishing it into a bold helmet, high above the long neck. I would like to see my friend Valentine retain her acid charm, which is part of her honest, gleaming blondeness, piquant, sharp and arched like a silver-gilt fork. I would like . . .

But that's not the case at all ! With ridiculous fervour she's performing before my eyes the rites ordained by Fashion ! Her hair comes down, lowers the height of her forehead, conceals her little childlike ears and the silvery nape of her neck. If the chin looks heavier as a result, and the neck shorter, it's nothing to do with me. . . . A skilful shading effect, ranging from white to crimson, covers the cheeks so richly that I feel like writing my name in it, with the tip of my nail, right in the powder. . . .

The maid slips the evening dress over the long elastic corset—a sort of complicated *zaïmph*, with layers of embroidery, painted, ruined and slashed into luxurious rags, one of them coming tightly across the bosom, the other over the knees, the third coming up in front over the length of the skirt, where it was fastened half-way up in the most odd and indiscreetly precise manner.

An artist in colour, with a heated, barbarous imagination, covered this fabric with orange and violet, the green of Venetian necklaces and the blue-black of sapphires, mingled with gold ; but a 'leader of fashion' pulled it all to pieces with the capriciousness of an evil and illiterate gnome. Then a woman came along—my friend Valentine—and cried 'I'm Scheherazade too—like everyone else !'

She preens herself before me, walking in a rhythmic, pigeon-toed fashion. She has weighed down her light blonde beauty with everything that would suit a sultana as pale and round as the moon. An Oriental jewel, a valuable one, in the shape of a tear, scintillates between her eyebrows, and is astonished that it can extinguish, with its brief flashes, two Western eyes of modest blue. . . . My friend has just fixed on top of her head, in addition, a long aigrette, made of stardust. . . .

The Peris, in the Persian paradise, wore this star on their foreheads and this wispy cloud. But my friend's feet vanish beneath a very Greek petticoat, with regular flowing pleats, clasped at the knees by a Hindu drapery. Her hand pulls into shape and arranges the square section of a Byzantine belt, with Egyptian beaded designs. . . .

Happy and serious, she admires herself, without suspecting that something is happening to her. . . . Something, good heavens, that happens to so many young, fair-complexioned Parisiennes, with slender noses and chins, with inadequate flesh and eyelashes, as soon as they disguise themselves as Asian princesses : she looks like a little housemaid.

*

My friend Valentine sat down, powdered the sides of her neck and the hollow above her chin, and after we had exchanged friendly, polite remarks, she was silent. I was surprised, for on the days when we have nothing to say to each other my friend Valentine elaborates easily on the theme 'Subjects of conversation are getting very rare !' during three-quarters of an hour of scintillating chat. . . .

She was silent, and I saw that something about the

carriage of her head had changed. With a slightly timid air she thrust her forehead towards me and looked at me from underneath. 'I've had my hair cut off,' she admitted all at once, and she removed her hat.

The lovely blonde hair at the nape of her neck showed where it had been recently cut and was still rebelling against the scissors, while from a parting on the left a full wave fell down over her forehead in Chateaubriand style.

'It doesn't suit me too badly, does it?' asked my friend with false courage.

'No, certainly not.'

'I'm just back from seeing the Hicks, they paid me lots of compliments, Monsieur Hicks said that I looked like . . . guess who?'

'Like someone convalescing from typhoid fever?'

'You're too kind, really. . . . But you haven't got it.'

'Like Dujardin-Beaumetz,[3] but more shorn? Like Drumont,[4] without spectacles?'

'Not him either. He said I looked like an English peeress, my dear!'

'Do the Hicks know any English peeresses?'

'You've evaded the question, as usual. Does it suit me or not?'

'It does. Very well, in fact. But I'm thinking of that long hair which is just so much dead golden grass, now . . . tell me, why have you had your hair cut, you too, like so many others?'

My friend Valentine shrugged her shoulders.

[3] Presumably the famous nineteenth-century French medical writer, Georges Dujardin-Beaumetz (1833–96).

[4] Edouard Drumont, the notorious French anti-Semite.

'How do I know? . . . It was just an idea. I couldn't stand myself with long hair any more. . . . And then, it's the fashion. In England, apparently . . .'

'Yes, yes, but what else?'

'Charlotte Lysès has certainly had hers cut,' she said evasively, 'And even Sorel[5] . . . I haven't seen her, but I've been told that she's wearing her hair "like a Roman gladiator". And Annie de Pène, and a hundred other women with good taste whose names I could quote to you, and . . .'

'And Polaire.'[6]

My friend paused in astonishment.

'Polaire? She hasn't got short hair.'

'I thought she had.'

'She has very long short hair. It's got nothing to do with the present fashion. Polaire wears her hair in her own style. When I had my hair cut I wasn't thinking of Polaire for one moment.'

'What were you thinking of? I'd like you to tell me why women have been stricken with this contagious disease : cutting their hair off level with their ears, when previously all this hair was cherished, waved and scented. . . .'

She rose impatiently and walked about, shaking her romantic lock.

'You're odd . . . I don't know. I couldn't stand my long hair any more, I tell you. And then it's hot. And then at night it pulled on my neck and got wrapped round one of my arms . . .'

---

[5] Cécile Sorel, one of the most famous French actresses of the twentieth century. She joined the Comédie-Française in 1901.

[6] Polaire, popular actress and music-hall star of Algerian origin, friend of Colette when they were both young and the star of *Claudine à Paris* in its 1902 stage version.

'Weren't you used to this fine plait after thirty years?'

'I imagine so. You ask me questions, I answer you, and that's because I'm kind-hearted. Just think, the other morning my plait got caught in a drawer which I'd closed quickly. I hate that. And then when we had air-raid warnings, it became absolute torture; nobody likes to look ghastly, even in a cellar, do they, with a chignon collapsing on one side and unravelling on the other. I could have died a thousand times because of that long hair. And also you can't reason about it. I've had my hair cut because I've had my hair cut.'

In front of the mirror she smoothed down her curls, and patted her 1830 wave into shape with a new type of gesture. How many freshly shorn women have invoked reasons of coquetry, the herd instinct, anglophilia—and even economy! —in order to explain away the same vandalism, before saying 'How do I know?'

'My neuralgia . . .' one of them would say.

'You know, I was tired of peroxide, I really had to renew my hair . . .' explained another one.

'It's cleaner,' a third one imagined. 'You can wash your hair while you're having your bath. . . .'

My friend Valentine did not support these modest truths with a new lie, but her attitude too is that of a prisoner who wants to break her fetters. I can amuse myself, therefore : as I look at the free coquetry of a head no longer weighed down with the coil of hair secured with pins, the pride of a forehead where the wind breaks up a slightly masculine curl, I can amuse myself seeing, or imagining, the delight of having shaken off an old fear that the war and the approach of the enemy had roused from a long oblivion, and the memory, barely conscious, of the desperate flight of women from the Barbarians when they ran naked and the flag of their hair, behind them, would suddenly knot round the wrists of their ravishers. . . .

*

I had written to my friend Valentine : 'Come over, we're going to the grape harvest.' She came, wearing flat-heeled canvas shoes and an autumn-coloured skirt; one bright green pullover, one pink one; a hat made of twill, another made of velvet, and both of them, as she said, 'invertebrate'. If she had not called a slug a snail and asked whether a bat was the female of a tawny owl, she wouldn't have been taken for a 'person from Paris'.

'The grape harvest?' she asked in astonishment. 'Really? In spite of the war?'

And I realized that deep within herself she was criticizing everything that this fine phrase grape harvest seemed to promise and recall of somewhat licentious liberty, singing and dancing, propositions and gourmandise. . . . Isn't there a traditional phrase 'the grape harvest celebrations'?

'In spite of the war, Valentine,' I admitted. 'What can they do? They haven't found a way of collecting the grapes without picking them. There are lots of grapes. We'll use flavoursome grapes and make several casks of wine that's drunk young and doesn't gain by ageing, the wine that's as harsh on the tongue as a swear-word. Peasants celebrate it as people praise boxers : "Strong, damn it !" since it hasn't any other virtues.'

It was so fine when we went to the grape harvest, it was so pleasant to linger on the way, that we didn't reach the hillside until ten o'clock, the time when the low hedges and the shady meadows were still wet with heavy dew, which was cold and blue-looking, while the strong Limousin sun already made our cheeks and necks tingle, warming the tardy peaches under their cotton plush, the securely hanging pears and the apples which were too heavy this year and torn off by a puff of wind. . . . My friend Valentine stopped by the ripe blackberries, the hairy scabious, even by the ears of maize, forcing off their dry husks and eating the grains like a young hen.

Like the guide in the desert who walks on ahead and promises the lagging traveller an oasis and a spring, I called out to her from far away : 'Come on, hurry up ! The grapes are better, and you'll drink the first wine from the vat, you'll have bacon and boiled chicken ! . . .'

Our entry into the vineyard caused no stir. There was plenty to do and, moreover, our clothes demanded neither curiosity nor even consideration. For her sacrifice to the blood of the grapes my friend had accepted my loan of an old check skirt which had known many ups and downs since 1914, while my personal elegance went no further than a smock-type apron in spotted satinette. A few tanned faces looked over the cordons of the vines, we were handed two empty baskets and we began work.

Since my friend Valentine was snipping off the grapes like a needlewoman, with delicate movements of her scissors, a jovial and silent faunlike old man stood up facing her, enjoyed giving her something of a fright, and then showed her without uttering a word how the bunch of grapes comes off the stock and falls into the basket, if one knows how to press on a secret suspension-point, which is revealed to the fingers by a little abscess, a swelling where the stem breaks like glass. A moment later Valentine was picking without scissors, as fast as her faunlike instructor, and since I didn't want her to do better or more than me the eleven o'clock sun soon made our skins moist and our tongues dry.

Who can have claimed that grapes can slake thirst? These were Limousin grapes grafted on to American stock, so ripe that their skins were crinkly, so sugary that they had a peppery taste, they stained our skirts and formed a crushed mass in our baskets, gave us a searing thirst and intoxicated the wasps. When Valentine rested from time to time on her feet, was she seeking on the hillside, among the well-regulated coming and going of people carrying baskets, both empty and full, the child cup-bearer who might have brought a jug of cold water? But the children carried only bunch after bunch, and the men—three old caryatids with withered muscles—carried only huge crimson-tinged wooden tubs towards the open storeroom at the farm at the bottom of the hill. . . .

The delight of the clear morning had gone. Noon is the austere moment when birds fall silent, when the shortened shadows crouch at the foot of the tree. A pall of heavy light crushed the slate roofs, flattened the hillside, smoothed out the shady fold of the valley. . . . I watched the melancholy and laziness of noon come down over my friend. She looked round about her, among the silent workers, for some gaiety that she might perhaps have criticized, some assistance—which she soon found.

The church bell ringing in some village was answered by murmurs of satisfaction, the clatter of sabots on the hardened pathways, and the distant shout 'Time for soup! Time for soup!'

Soup? Much more and much better than soup, in the shelter of a hangar of reeds draped with cream-coloured sheets, fastened together with twigs bearing green acorns,

blue convolvulus and pumpkin flowers. Soup and all its vegetables, yes, but boiled chicken too, top ribs of beef, bacon as
pink and white as a breast, veal in its natural juices. When
the smell of this feast reached my friend's nostrils she smiled
in that unconscious expansive way, with the smile you see in
babies who have had their fill of milk and women who are
satiated with pleasure. . . .

She sat down like a queen, in the place of honour, folded
her red-stained skirt beneath her, turned back her sleeves
and in cavalier fashion held out her glass to her neighbour
for him to fill it, with a youthful laugh. I saw by the look on
her face that she was going to call him 'my good man'. . . .
But she looked at him, fell silent and turned towards the man
on her left, then towards me as though to ask for help and
advice. The fact was that country protocol had seated her
between two grape harvesters who between them carried the
weight of a hundred and sixty-six years and were slightly
bent beneath so much. One was thin, dried up and transparent, with bluish eyes and wispy hair, living in the silence
of an elderly sprite. The other, who was still a giant, with
bones as big as cudgels, cultivated a piece of land all on his
own, boasting in advance, as though defying death, about
the asparagus he would get from it 'in four or five years'
time'!

I noticed the moment when Valentine, between her two
old men, was losing her cheerfulness, and I had a litre of
cider taken to her by a page who was likely to amuse her,
one of those broadly smiling boys, slightly plump for his
sixteen years, just as handsome—with his submissive, crafty
forehead, his yellow eyes and Arab nose—as the much-
vaunted Italian shepherds. She smiled at him, without
giving him much attention, for she was suddenly preoccu-

pied with statistics. She asked the ethereal old man and then the strong octogenarian their ages. She leant forward to ask that of another curly-headed and wrinkled worker, who only admitted to seventy-three years. She learnt other equally remarkable figures from the far ends of the table—sixty-eight and seventy-one—began to mutter to herself, to add up lustra and centuries, and was laughed at by a jolly woman with five children who shouted to her from where she sat, 'So you like them like wine, then, with cobwebs on the cork !'

The result was laughter from old and young, remarks in dialect and also in extremely clear French, which made my friend blush and renewed her appetite. She wanted some more bacon, and cut some of the illicit bread, kneaded from pure barley, brown but succulent, and demanded from the muscular giant an account of the war of 1870. It was brief.

'What can I say? It wasn't a very pretty sight . . . I remember that everyone round me fell and died in their own blood. . . . Nothing happened to me. . . . Not one bullet, not one bayonet thrust. I was left standing, and they were on the ground. . . . Who knows why?'

He fell into indifferent silence, and the women round us grew gloomy. Until then no mother deprived of her son, no sister accustomed to do double work because of her absent brother, had mentioned the war or the men who were absent, nor groaned from the exhaustion of three years. . . . The farmer's wife was tight-lipped as she busily gave out thick glasses for coffee, but she said nothing about her son, the artilleryman. A grey-haired and very weary farmer, whose stomach was propped up with a truss, said not a word about his four sons : one was eating roots in Germany, two were fighting, the fourth slept beneath ground that had been ripped by machine-guns. . . .

'All this war,' said a very old woman seated on a truss of straw not far from the table, 'is the fault of the barons . . .'

'The barons?' asked Valentine, who was very interested. 'What barons?'

'The barons of France,' said the cracked voice. 'And those of Germany! All wars have been the fault of the barons.'

'In what way?'

My friend looked at her avidly, as though she were hoping that the black rags would disappear and the woman would stand up in hennin and vair, crying 'I am the fourteenth century!' but nothing of the kind occurred, the old woman merely shook her head, and all that could be heard were the drunken, confident wasps, the puffing of a distant train, and the gums of the transparent old man chewing. . . .

However, I had broken the maize galette into pieces, and the tepid coffee was still in the glasses when the grape harvesters already began to turn away towards the burning hillside.

'What?' said the astonished Valentine, 'No siesta?'

'Yes, there is, but only for you and me. Come under the filbert trees, we can let ourselves melt gently with heat and sleep. The wheat harvest allows a siesta, but not the grape harvest. You see, they're at work already. . . .'

It wasn't true, for the file of men and women going up the hill had stopped, looking at something.

'What are they looking at?'

'Someone's coming through the field . . . two ladies. They're making signs to the workers. . . . They know them. Have you invited any of your country neighbours?'

'Not one. But wait, I think I know that blue dress. But. . . . But . . . it's . . .'

'They're. . . . Yes, of course!'

With an unhurried, coquettish air they walked forward, one wearing a straw hat, the other carrying a white sunshade : our two maids. Mine wore small khaki-coloured kid shoes and above them was a swaying blue-serge skirt which emphasized the saffron-coloured lawn of her blouse. The soubrette who looked after my friend was all in mauve and the openwork sleeves allowed a glimpse of her bare arms, while her belt, in white suède to match her shoes, was clasped round a waist which fashion might perhaps have preferred less slender. . . .

From our hiding-place in the shade we saw ten men run up to them, twenty hands hailed them on the steep slope, while envious little girls carried their sunshades. The elderly giant suddenly became animated, seated one maid on an empty grape-tub and hoisted the whole thing on to his shoulders; a handsome, sunburnt adolescent smelt a handkerchief taken away from one of the two young women. . . . The heavy air seemed light to them, now that the feminine, affected laughter of two women, deliberately prolonged, rang through it. . . .

'They've set out to look attractive, my goodness!' murmured my friend Valentine. 'It's my mauve Dinard dress of three years ago. She's remade the front at the top . . .'

'Really?' I said, half-aloud. 'Louise is wearing my serge skirt of two years ago. I would never have believed it could look so new. At that time one could still find splendid serge. . . . I can't think why on earth I gave her my yellow blouse ! I could use it on Sundays, this year. . . .'

I looked involuntarily at my spotted smock apron, and I saw Valentine contemptuously fingering my old check shirt, with its grapejuice stains. Above us, on the scorching hot hillside, the mauve young woman and the yellow one were

walking along among flattering laughter and exclamations
of satisfaction. The elegance, the Parisian quality, the aristocratic dignity which we had removed from the grape harvest
were no longer missing, thanks to them, and for them the
rough workers became once more gallant, youthful and
audacious. . . .

A man who knelt, invisible, between the vine stocks raised
towards our maids a branch laden with blue grapes, and
both of them, instead of filling baskets, helped themselves.

Then they spread out their handkerchiefs and sat down
on the edge of a slope with their sunshades open, to watch
the grape harvest, and beneath their benevolent, idle gaze
everyone rivalled each other in ardour.

Our silence had lasted a long time when my friend Valentine broke it with these words, unworthy no doubt of the
great thought they expressed: 'Well, now. . . . Roll on
feudalism!'

*

In my friend Valentine's Restoration boudoir—for her the
'Restoration' period embraces in generous and anachronistic
fashion the fifteenth century, the Directorate, the Second
Empire and even the Grévy style—there's a little picture by
Velvet Breughel. Snow turned into smoked gold, a little
house with a pointed roof radiating miraculous beams of
light, and, converging on the house, strings of gnomes in fur
caps—in short a *Nativity* by Velvet Breughel, what an art
dealer calls 'a nice little knick-knack' or a 'marvellous little
picture', depending on whether he is good-natured or distinguished.

At my friend Valentine's place I often drink tea, which I

don't like, while looking at the Velvet Breughel, which I do.

'Valentine,' I asked my friend yesterday, in an absent-minded way, 'where did that little picture come from?'

She blushed.

'Why do you ask me that?'

'I didn't think I was being indiscreet.'

She blushed even more deeply.

'Of course not! Not in the slightest. . . . It's a family memento. It was given to me in 1913 by my aunt Poittier.'

'Your aunt Poittier? Which one? You have as many aunts and uncles named Poittier as there are seeds in a water-melon.'

She fidgeted uneasily.

'Yes, that's true. Must you really remind me of this story, in which I played a part that was . . .'

'Dishonest?'

'Almost. You won't leave me in peace until I've told you the story, will you? In 1913 my aunt Poittier . . .'

'Which one?'

'Aunt Olga. You don't know her. In 1913 my aunt Poittier lost her only son . . .'

'A little boy, if I remember rightly?'

'Yes, a little boy of about forty-eight. Then, since there was no longer anything to keep her in Chartres, she came to live in Paris with my uncle Poittier. They settled in the rue Raynouard, but as they felt very lonely they spent nearly all their time with the Poittier uncle . . .'

'Which one?'

'The one living in the place d'Iéna, Paul Poittier, the brother. . . . But I told you you didn't know him! And since Aunt Marie lived in the boulevard Delessert at that time . . .'

'Who was Aunt Marie?'

'Oh, Aunt Marie Poittier, let's see, the third brother's wife, you don't know her! If you will keep on interrupting me . . .'

'I won't say another word.'

'. . . So they were very glad they could visit their neighbours as they wished; it was useful for me when I made my monthly round of family visits. In 1913 I'd gone to spend the Easter holidays with the Charles's . . .'

'Which Charles's? Charles Poittier?'

'No, the Charles Loisillons.'

'Oh, good, I prefer that.'

'Why?'

'I like those Loisillons, among the confusing mass of Poittiers like a poplar tree on an empty plain. Go on, please.'

'What was I saying? Oh yes. . . . So, at the Charles's I received a telegram from Mama: UNCLE DIED YESTERDAY. FUNERAL TOMORROW. ASSEMBLE PLACE D'IÉNA, TOMORROW MORNING, TEN O'CLOCK PRECISELY. I borrowed my cousin Charles's crape veil, black cloak and black gloves and rushed for the train, travelling overnight. I reached the house of mourning half an hour late, after a night on the train, with an empty stomach, wearing my crape veil. . . . I could hardly see or stand, and then as soon as I began to go upstairs there was that smell of crushed flowers. . . . In Aunt Olga's big drawing-room there sat a wall of women, veiled from head to foot in thick crape. I began to kiss them all and murmured "Oh, poor Uncle . . . can you believe it. . . ." One is so stupid when one is not upset, isn't one?'

'All the same I recognized Mama's good, firm hand, and her violet scent, and I clung to her skirt as I had done when I was little. I said to her very quietly "But how did it happen?" She had no time to reply, for another black wall, taller this time, the phalanx of men in full mourning, began to move towards us, and we stood up. Uncle Edme . . .'

'Who's Uncle Edme?'

'A distant uncle . . . you don't know him—came to kiss me, and then another cousin, and then two schoolboys wearing woollen gloves, and other relatives, and finally a tall, dried-up old man, with red eyes, who kissed my hand and said to me: "My dear niece, how good of you to come back. . . ." He looked up: I uttered a loud yell and collapsed into someone's arms.'

'Why?'

'The dead man was in front of me, wearing a white tie, thanking me for having come back. . . . Come back! And what about him, then! I was taken away, unconscious, and I only recovered when I learnt that I had got the wrong uncle, that the real dead man had died of an embolism at his brother's house and they hadn't brought him to the rue Raynouard and . . .'

'I see. But how does the little Velvet Breughel picture come into all this?'

My friend shrugged her shoulders.

'Well, you can imagine how my hysteria and fainting fit upset the ceremony. My mother fanned me, gave me smelling-salts and said to Aunt Olga, the dead uncle's wife . . .'

'The wrong uncle?'

'No, the right one! Good heavens, how irritating you are! and she said to Aunt Olga: "It's grief . . . shock . . . my poor little daughter is so sensitive, so affectionate. . . ."

'A month later Aunt Olga sent me the Breughel "in memory"—I still feel ashamed—"in memory of Uncle Poittier whom his little Valentine loved so much". What was I to do? Admit I'd got the uncles mixed up? I kept the Breughel. It's so pretty. . . .'

My friend took her table napkin, gently wiped the gilded snow in the *Nativity* and heaved a sigh in which I tried to find as much remorse as delectation.

VIRAGO MODERN CLASSICS

The first Virago Modern Classic, *Frost in May* by Antonia White, was published in 1978. It launched a list dedicated to the celebration of women writers and to the rediscovery and reprinting of their works. Its aim was, and is, to demonstrate the existence of a female tradition in fiction which is both enriching and enjoyable, and to broaden the sometimes narrow academic definition of a 'classic' which has often led to the neglect of a large number of interesting secondary works of fiction. In calling the series 'Modern Classics' we do not necessarily mean 'great' — although this is often the case. Published with new critical and biographical introductions, books are chosen for many reasons: sometimes for their importance in literary history; sometimes because they illuminate particular aspects of women's lives, both personal and public. They may be classics of comedy or storytelling; their interest can be historical, feminist, political or literary.

Initially the Virago Modern Classics concentrated on English novels and short stories published in the early decades of this century. As the series has grown it has broadened to include works of fiction from different centuries, different countries, cultures and literary traditions, many of which have been suggested by our readers.